WRUSH

by: The Karakul

To Adam,
Best wishes
& Karakul

Tabetha's Last Task

VOLUME TWO

BY THE KARAKUL

Tinderbox Press

Published by Tinderbox Press
Edmonton, AB
www.TheSecretWorlds.com

Distributed by Secret Worlds Productions, Ltd.

For ordering information or special discounts for bulk purchases, please visit www.TheSecretWorlds.com

Design and composition by Greenleaf Book Group LLC and Alex Head
Illustration and cover design by Ruke (www.RukeStudios.com)

Publisher's Cataloging-In-Publication Data
(Prepared by The Donohue Group, Inc.)
Karakul.
    Wrush / by the Karakul. — 1st ed.
    v. ; cm. — (Tabetha's Last Task)
    Summary: A young girl who is confined to a wheelchair receives a magical pen and is able to draw herself into the enchanted world of Wrush where she will become the empress. A magical adventure ensues.
    ISBN: 978-1-934572-38-2 (v. 1)
    ISBN: 978-1-937110-10-9 (v. 2)
    1. Children with disabilities—Juvenile fiction. 2. Empresses—Juvenile fiction. 3. Children with disabilities—Fiction. 4. Empresses—Fiction. 5. Fantasy. 6. Fantasy fiction. I. Title.
    PZ7.K127 Wr 2010
    [Fic]

Part of the Tree Neutral® program, which offsets the number of trees consumed in the production and printing of this book by taking proactive steps, such as planting trees in direct proportion to the number of trees used: www.treeneutral.com

TreeNeutral

Printed in Canada on acid-free paper

11 12 13 14 15 16   10 9 8 7 6 5 4 3 2 1

First Edition

Part One

Author's Note

You may not like what I am about to say, reader.

You may think me a scoundrel or a wretch. You may shout, "He's tricked us! He should have warned us back in Book One!" But alas, my friends, if I had told you then what I am about to now, I believe courage would have fled you like rats before a flood, and the story of Tabetha Bright would remain unread.

You see, there are many secrets lurking at the edges of our world. Each is revealed in its own time. If I have waited till now to speak of this one, it is because only now are you ready. So I tell you:

This book is not at all what it seems.

Yes, this is it, my secret in full. But many great things are packed into such tiny words. Many extraordinary wonders. I will now list them.

To begin with, this book will feel deceptively light in your hands. If you doubt me, lift it once or twice in the air.

I mean it. Lift the book in the air.

That's right. Now try the other hand.

Do I lie?

Of course not. You will find this book's weight easy to handle, no more cumbersome than a hat, and yet in this matter you are greatly deceived. The true weight of this book, unbelievable as it may seem, goes far beyond the measure of man!

Furthermore, if you sit quietly enough, or perhaps sleep with it under your pillow, you may notice a sound coming straight off the pages. It is much like a hum or a vibration. If you touch the book at these times you may feel a slight tingle, or in the most extreme cases, an electric shock.

No! Do not be alarmed. It happens only rarely. I have experienced it myself and it has caused me little damage.

The point I am making is this: You hold before you a collection of pages, each decorated with ink, and you rightly expect to find a story nestled somewhere within. In this much, I admit, you are correct. But what is contained within these pages is more than just a story, for it does what few stories can do. It *will change you.* That's right. You will become a different person by the end, seeing the world through different eyes, and if this upsets you I suggest you stop reading at once.

However, if you count yourself among the adventurous of this world, if you believe broken hearts break also new trails— even if you are simply curious, and wish to test the truth of my challenge then I am afraid you have no choice but to read on. A journey like no other has been tucked into these pages.

My name is The Karakul.

"It's a lonely thing keeping a secret all to yourself."

*N*ow for this story to begin, my dear reader, I require you to imagine a hospital. Not a nice hospital. Not a fresh new clinic with flowers, and laughter, and gleaming white floors. No, an old hospital; a ten-story ruin, bent as a hag, crooked as her teeth, with an oily black breath wheezing up from its pipes like the unholy smoke of factories. And once the hideousness of this place has been erected in your mind, I must next ask you to enter. Yes, to brave its dimly lit hallways that reek of ammonia and mold. To creep past its tired walls and sagging ceilings, then down a flight of damp steps to the end of a long corridor, where a solitary ray of light pushes through the small, dusty window and falls across the cheek of an eight-year-old girl, alone in her wheelchair, as she writes on the clean white pages of her notebook . . .

Tabetha Bright set down her pen, shaking out the cramps

in her fingers. Her hand burned and ached like a slow-roasted claw, for she had been writing all morning. She had filled page after page until her eyes blinked with the strain and still, *it wasn't working*. Her magic pen wasn't doing its magic.

Here was yet another story she had written about the three enchanted pyramids she must find, one of a dozen tales Tabetha kept tucked away in her dresser. The magic of her pen should have taken her straight to the first pyramid, but it hadn't. She had no idea why.

Tabetha glanced out the window, catching her reflection as she did so. For as long as she'd been ill, she had been pale and frail, small and weak. The nurses often jokes that they had to shake out the sheets to find her in bed, but in this moment Tabetha was nevertheless shocked to see just how little weight was left on her. Her brown eyes, which had always been large, appeared enormous and overly bright in the window's glare. Her delicate features were more delicate, her narrow shoulders narrower. Her blue pajamas hung from her like a gown. On the whole, Tabetha appeared sickly, and after months in the hospital, doing her best to recover from several bouts of pneumonia, the disappointment of getting sicker was hard to ignore.

"And look who's still writing in that notebook!"

Tabetha slammed her book shut, the clap of its pages echoing down the long corridor. The voice belonged to the big nurse, the one who smelled like sausages and perfume. She strode toward Tabetha all smiles and lipstick, her enormous, bushy red hair bouncing with each step. In the wheelchair before her, the nurse pushed a boy.

At first glance, there was nothing unusual about the boy. He had raven-black hair and dark, shining eyes. He was older than Tabetha, perhaps eleven or twelve, of average height, and with fine features. Yet Tabetha knew he was much more than just a boy. Thomas Morlac, behind the pouting displays and quick flashes of anger, was a sorcerer. A very talented sorcerer, who at a very young age had mastered the art of magic and taken it to entirely new hieghts. The only problem was that his heart had gone black. Unable to walk, and unable to forgive the world for his misfortune, Thomas burned with a blistering fury that fueled the dark craft of his sorcery. He was the arch-enemy of Wrush, and all other magical worlds. Worst of all, Thomas was Tabetha's roommate.

Thomas scowled hatefully as the nurse pushed him past. Whether the scowl was meant for her, or the weird stink of the nurse, Tabetha couldn't yet tell. She released the brakes on her own wheelchair, following the nurse into the dimness of their bedroom. Within were two dreary beds, matching dressers, a dreary lamp. Everything, in fact, became dreary in Thomas's presence, as if a dark cloud were about him, and nothing withstood the blackness of his mood. Tabetha suspected that even the hospital— the building itself— which had once been sunny and bright, had succumbed to Thomas's foul touch and fallen into its present state of disrepair. Within their bedroom there were, however, two large windows— one for each bed— and it was this alone that made sharing space with Thomas bearable.

In her friendly way, the big nurse grumbled: "Don't you ever get tired, Tabetha? Write, write, write. That's all you ever do. And then Thomas with his notebooks and his pen flying right beside you. You'd think there was some kind of race between you two. Well, he's back from therapy now, and he did a good job today. Coming along very quickly, aren't you Thomas? Keep it up and you'll be walking again in no time!"

Tabetha had heard it was car accident that had injured Thomas, putting him in the hospital wing for children who couldn't walk. But he would never speak of it himself. Thomas glared down at his legs as the nurse wheeled him to the window near his bed. The nurse paid his anger no notice, jabbering merrily to herself as she attached the tray to Thomas's wheelchair and then set him up with his own notebooks and pens.

"There you are now!" she said as she finished, then turned to Tabetha. "How about you dear? Need anything before I go?"

Tabetha shook her head vigorously, her brown hair whipping about her shoulders.

"Fine, fine, just holler if you do!" Then she swooshed out of the room with her huge old-nurse hips swinging side-to-side and her awful old-nurse perfume suffocating Tabetha like bug spray. Tabetha tried to hold her breath till it passed, and her cheeks puffed up, her eyes bulging like a fish, but then her throat got that tickle . . .

And she coughed.

She coughed hard.

She coughed till she was red in the face.

She coughed till her ears rang, till her stomach was sore, till her eyes caught fire with tears. She coughed and she coughed, shaking her head, fighting for air, catching it at last, then rubbed her chest, which was burning, cleared her throat, smiled, feeling a little embarrassed, and then glanced at Thomas Morlac who surprised her with a matching grin.

His grin was tight as a zipper, for he was trying to hide it, trying not to laugh (because that would completely ruin his anger) but Tabetha saw that smile all the same.

She would never forget it either.

"That stuff is like bathroom deodorizer!" she joked as she rubbed the ache in her chest, expecting Thomas to break down and laugh at last. She knew he wanted to. "How did you ever make it down the hall and back without choking on that nurse's perfume?"

Instead of laughter, an uncomfortable silence followed.

Tabetha listened to the steady click of someone in high-heels going down the long hall. Then the soft rustle of Thomas's clothing as he turned from her with a dramatic twist of the shoulders. He began digging through his box of pens as if no smile had been shared between them.

Nothing's changed, Tabetha thought as she puffed the hair from her eyes, wondering once again if she was just wasting her time trying to befriend him. Of course she wasn't, and deep down she knew this, for a sincere effort is never wasted. And if I have not said so before, I will say it now: Friendship is like a live ember. It will only smother if kept hidden, but if given lively attention it will ignite and warm us.

Tabetha's greatest difficulty was in getting Thomas to see this truth. So much depended on the two of them making peace. But clever as she was, she knew that peace with the dark sorcerer would not come easy. She had no trouble seeing the peculiarity of their situation. Tabetha was the empress of an enchanted empire called Wrush, with an army of her own, and Thomas was her most dreaded enemy. So strange that they should be sitting here now, mere children in a hospital, facing each other in their wheelchairs as if the fate of the universe did not hang in the balance.

"It's Gwybies you're writing about, isn't it," she said, noticing Thomas's own magic pen, which was identical to her own, scribbling across his paper. Gwybies were the hideous creatures Thomas had created back in Wrush, and they answered to his every beck and call. "You're always writing about Gwybies so you can try to bring the whole army of them over here."

Thomas's pen halted, and there was a moment of silence. Then the scratching of his pen resumed.

"I know it's true," Tabetha said. "I know that's why you never show anyone your stories. But how come it doesn't work? How come the magic pen doesn't pull your Gwybies here to Earth?"

He paused again, looking up this time. "How do you know it doesn't?"

"Because your Gwybies would be here already," she said, then added, "And I would already be at the first pyramid."

The pyramid she spoke of was one of three that had been scattered across the universe long ago. Known as the Three Guardians, their magic formed a wall, like an enormous electric net, that protected Earth from the rest of the universe. And Thomas Morlac planned to tear that wall down.

"So that's what you've been writing about, then," he snorted. "The Three Pyramids?"

Tabetha nodded. "You must have known, I leave my stories out in plain sight. Besides, it only makes sense. You know I plan to find each of the Three Pyramids before you, and my magic pen seems the quickest way. Only it's not working like it used to."

She paused. "Thomas . . . tell me why."

He touched his thumb to his nose and sniffed. "Why should I?"

"Because you know. Because you know why I can't write my way to the pyramids, and why you can't write your Gwybies here to Earth, and deep down inside, I think you actually want to tell me. It's a lonely thing keeping a secret all to yourself."

Thomas appeared to think for a long time before answering. He played with the pen's cap, snapping it open and closed. With a final click, he set the pen down on the tray and said, "The magic in the pens is fading. Soon, they'll even run out of ink, just like any other pen."

"What?"

This was terrible! Tabetha had never even considered the possibility. "Can we still write our way back to Wrush?"

Hesitantly, the boy nodded. "Only there's certain things we can't do with the pens anymore."

Tabetha glanced at her story. "Like write my way directly to the pyramids."

"Or write my Gwybies directly to Earth." He looked at her and added, "There's something else too. Before, the magic pens could actually create more of Wrush, could add to it. That's how

Wrush first came to be. That's how I made the Gwybies. But as the magic runs dry, we're able to do less and less. These two pens are the last of them. When their magic ink runs out, there is no more. Nothing. Nobody will be crossing the Hedge again."

The Hedge being the name for that wall between worlds, that magic blue net, and Tabetha thought: *Unless, of course, you manage to destroy the Hedge.* Though Thomas never said so aloud, she knew this was his plan. Absurd as it seems, he had gone so far as to make a 'to do' list for conquering the universe, which she had seen just yesterday among his bedside stacks. It read as follows:

1. Find the Three Pyramids, which are scattered and hidden throughout the universe

2. Control their magic, which activates the Hedge: the wall between worlds

3. Shut down the Hedge, which will bring down the wall and leave Earth unprotected

4. Wait for Pump Dragons, who are always searching for their Noble Fruit, to dig fresh Wink Holes, or pathways, to Earth

5. Lead my army of Gwybies through

6. Conquer Earth, heart of the universe

A more terrible list Tabetha had never seen, but in the end it all boiled down to one thing: She had to get to the pyramids. It was that simple. She had to find all three, and most importantly, she had to find all three pyramids *before* her roommate.

"Thomas, I need to know one more thing."

His head was down, pen scratching away. "No."

Tabetha sighed, nodding slowly to herself. It was a start, anyway. At least Thomas had told her this much, which was more than he'd ever said to her before. In a way, she actually felt a bit of hope, perhaps for the first time since discovering her roommate was in fact an evil sorcerer bent on conquering every light in the sky.

"Thomas?"

Surprisingly, he looked up this time, and met her eyes.

"Thank you," she said.

𝓛

Tabetha sat thinking for a long time, rolling Thomas's words around her mind like a ball. She watched him write, listened to the sound of his pen across paper. At some point her gaze drifted to the window, suddenly dazzled by the view beyond. The leaves were changing. Her eyes flitted from one tree to the next, drinking in their bold light: red, yellow, green, orange. On this misty breath of a morning, the sky an electric grey, Tabetha considered the spray of colors before her with a seriousness, an urgency, a depth of concentration that went beyond the mere eight years of her life.

Tabetha wheeled closer to the window, her skin recoiling from its chill. There was a faint smell of mildew where water seeped under the sill, but Tabetha didn't mind. She'd often heard the nurses complaining about this weather, competing with one another's stories of ailments; so many creaking joints angered by the bitter dampness of this building. Just this morning, before Tabetha had even awoken, a particularly grumpy nurse had stormed into her room with the express purpose of throwing open the curtain and crying out, "Gruesome! Gruesome! Nothing more gruesome than grey skies through a window!"

And yet, peering through that very same window now, Tabetha saw a swirl of color, a season in bloom. Why was that? Why should sky and leaves look so different to her? And for that matter, what *was* beauty when two people couldn't agree?

She didn't know. There was so much she didn't know, and yet knowing this, strangely, made one decision all the more clear:

Tabetha had to go back to Wrush.

No more wasting time (and magic ink) trying to write her way directly to the first pyramid. She needed to get back to Wrush, and as quickly as possible. Her friends there were sure to help her find the pyramid. Tabetha removed the magic pen from the spiral rings of her notebook. She clicked its top, and the glowing tip emerged. At the sound, Thomas set down his own pen.

"Now what are you doing?"

"Going back," she said.

Their wheelchairs faced each other, barely ten paces apart.

"Why bother going back?" Thomas asked. "I have the Pyramid Map. You won't find any pyramids without it."

Tabetha couldn't help but grin. *He doesn't know,* she thought. *He doesn't know I have a copy too, right on the back of the sun-wyrm's head!*

"I'm going back," she said again, more determined this time. "I plan to find the first pyramid and do whatever I can to protect it from you. There's no way I'll let you tear the Hedge down, Thomas."

He picked up his pen again. "Unless I get there first," he said.

Out of nowhere, Tabetha felt that same tickle in her throat. She coughed once or twice, small coughs, and then swallowed hard.

Thomas smirked again, but this time with cruelty. "It's your pneumonia, Tabetha. You're getting sicker."

She folded her arms and frowned. "Be quiet."

"We've both heard the doctors talking," he continued. "I'm learning to walk again. You're just getting worse. Your pneumonia isn't going away like they said it would."

Tabetha scowled, trying to be angry and not cry.

"You're not going to Wrush, Tabetha," Thomas said. "Not before noon anyway. Your medicine doesn't get here till noon. Leave without it and you might even—"

"True for you too, Thomas," she interrupted, not wanting to hear him say the word out loud. "You may be getting stronger, but you still need your medicine at noon too."

He stared. "Then I guess neither of us is going anywhere. Not until our medicine arrives."

Barely a moment passed before the smell of sausages and perfume wafted under the door. "Hello hello children! Twelve o'clock!" came the bushy-haired nurse's voice before she barged into the room carrying water and two small paper cups filled with pills. "Time for your meds, Thomas!" She set one cup of pills on his wheelchair's tray, poured a glass of water. Thomas's eyes remained fixed on Tabetha.

"And yours, my dear." The nurse poured another cup of water for Tabetha, and set the pills by her hand. The nurse floated out of the room without another word, leaving Thomas and Tabetha face-to-face, each with a magic pen in one fist and a cup of pills beside the other.

Silence.

Tabetha felt her muscles grow rigid. She willed her eyes not to blink.

Thomas made statues appear restless.

The silence built and stretched, the big clock above the door tick-ticking like a hammer in Tabetha's ears.

Then it happened.

Thomas moved for his cup of pills, Tabetha grabbed for hers. Thomas tossed his pills back, took a mouthful of water. Tabetha reached for her cup and bumped it. Her fingertips sent the cup over the edge of her wheelchair's tray, the little orange pills scattering across the floor.

No!

The air jumped from her lungs. Her chest squeezed tight. "Nooooo," she whined softly, her throat aching and stiff. "No please . . . not my medicine . . ." The pills were gone, scattered like mice. Nearly frantic, Tabetha's eyes darted around the room, searching for any hint of orange.

There!

She found one, caught right beneath the rear tire of her wheelchair. It was only one pill, but if she could just . . .

Tabetha leaned down over her wheelchair's side, hoping to snag the pill, or even brush it out from under the big wheel. She stretched. So close. Reaching and straining, she grunted, and then lunged, the movement rocking her wheelchair and rolling it ever so slightly forward . . . and crushing the pill underneath.

Devastated, Tabetha sat back up.

Thomas was gone.

Tabetha slumped in her chair, head down. She felt her chin begin to quiver, her eyes begin to sting. Thomas was on his way to Wrush, maybe even there already. He wouldn't wait around for Tabetha to catch up. He would get his map, gather his army of Gwybies and head straight for the first pyramid at once.

He would win, and just as painful right now, *he was right*.

Tabetha knew she was getting sicker. It wasn't hard to figure out. She also knew Thomas was getting stronger, but did he have to say it? He was already going to win, to find the first pyramid before her, but did he have to remind her what every doctor had been whispering? That even with her medicine, chances were, she probably wouldn't live long enough to see another . . .

Tabetha didn't realize she was crying till the first tear slipped from her chin.

"Oh , dear, dear," came a familiar voice from behind. "Did your little friend go off without you? Poor little Tabetha. I know it can be lonely here in the hospital, but there's no need to cry."

Tabetha sniffed and wiped her eyes. "It's not that," she said to the smiling nurse. "I spilled my medicine. I can't find it any-where."

"Is that all?" The nurse's lipstick was bright as wet candy. Her cheeks were powdery orange. "Well just wait right here," she said in her cheerful voice. "I'll be back with more."

The nurse hurried away, the squeak of her footsteps fading into silence, and Tabetha couldn't help but smile to herself. "What is beauty?" she had asked herself earlier that morning. Well now she knew, because the stink of old sausages and per-fume had never smelled prettier.

"Dragon's oil! Dragon's oil here!"

So, little Tabetha waited for her medicine. And time passed slowly, the way it always does when you are waiting and the second-hand on the clock seems to be faking a limp. It was not easy, this waiting. Just imagine, dear reader, a small flame beneath your seat, and you will have some notion of the restlessness she endured. Tabetha whimpered and squirmed, ground her teeth till they squeaked, wrung her hands and picked the gum from her wheels. Had the nurse forgotten her? What could be taking so long?

When the huge lady finally returned, pills in hand, Tabetha nearly bolted from her seat. She thanked the nurse, and hugged her, as best she could from the hold of her wheelchair.

"Well!" chuckled the nurse in surprise. "It's just a cup of pills, Tabetha!"

"I know." Tabetha squeezed tighter. "Thanks, though. A lot."

Tabetha let go and accepted the cup. Without waiting, she emptied it into her mouth. The orange pills made a sticky clump and it took four sips of water to get them down, but after her upset, Tabetha thought they tasted sweeter than a spoonful of honey. "I think I'll take a nap now," she told the nurse in a wobbly voice, her breath still snagging on the hooks of sadness. "I think I'll pull the curtains around my bed, too."

The big nurse winked. "Don't you worry, Tabetha. Nobody's going to come bother you till you're good and ready. You have my word. Now go on, get some rest."

Tabetha wheeled to her bed. She grabbed the siderails and with a small grunt hauled herself onto the mattress. She sniffled one last time, wiped her nose with the back of her hand and then exhaled long and slow, feeling the last of her sorrow wash away.

She pulled the curtains around her bed.

Despite her distress, the closing of the curtains marked the beginning of an excitement, a warm tingle that started low in her belly. It grew stronger as she took out her magic pen. Thomas was gone, but if she hurried, she just might catch up. Tabetha slipped a piece of paper from her stack on the bedstand, and without a moment to lose, she began to write.

Tabetha wrote about Wink Holes and Grimpkins and bowls of Dream Butter. She described her friends, Isaac, Answer, and the Mungling— by far the best part of Wrush. She described the floating city of Etherios and the Cloud Shepherd and his sheep. She described the Citadel that held her throne.

Slowly at first, as though swept away by a dream, Tabetha

watched her words take on life, then start to grow on their own. Her vision began to blur like thick jelly. She felt this world's grip loosen and another take hold as strange colors shocked her eyes, new sensations pinched her heart, and all the bustling sounds of a city crowded about her.

"Dragon's oil! Dragon's oil here!"

Outside.

Yes, she was outside, in a narrow, crowded lane somewhere. Perhaps it was a market, or a carnival.

"Hair-fruit! Freshest around! Shave one while they're ripe!"

Shouting and waving, laughter and the smells of cooking. Tabetha still sat upon her bed, pillow across her lap, but everywhere she looked, swarms of people hustled by or hollered from stalls. Crowds poured around her bed like a river, flowing down the lane. *Yes, a market*, she realized. Tabetha was in Wrush, at the Hubbub Bazaar in the old quarter of the floating city of Etherios.

"Frowns here! Get your frowns!"

High above the brightly colored awnings and the crooked little shops, the blue sun of Wrush burned silent and clear. The sun's scent, which washed over Wrush each day until nightfall, was like that of the tiniest flower when it has grown right through a wall and bloomed in the face of the impossible.

"Half price for you, Your Majesty. No better frown than these here. Take a look." A man with a tremendous grin leaned over Tabetha's bed. He was bald as a bowling ball with a red mustache so long it was tucked behind his ears. His eyes squinted into glittering crescents when he smiled, which seemed to be all the time. He reached back into his wagon and selected a jar of purple liquid. He held it out, and looking closer, Tabetha saw the shapes of little lips appear and disappear. Appear and disappear.

Little *frowns*, by the look of them.

She pointed. "Those are really . . .?"

"Frowns, Your Majesty. Yes, indeedy. Highest quality around, they be."

Tabetha peered closer at the jar, wrinkling her nose.

"I have them shipped in fresh from Gorgonport each week. Interest you in bottle, perhaps?" Somehow, the man's huge smile stretched wider, his eyes like sparkling slits. "Got them in larger sizes as well, Your Majesty."

"I don't understand," said Tabetha, genuinely bewildered. "I mean . . . what would I do with a frown?" She'd heard stories of the strange and magical items sold here in the Hubbub Bazaar. She shook the jar a bit, watching the lips kissing themselves tight against the glass, holding best as they could while the purple liquid swirled around. She lifted the jar above her head and had a look from beneath. "Don't you think smiles would be nicer? Certainly people would pay more for a smile."

"They do! They do!" The strange man's eyes shut completely in his excitement. "Bought me out completely, they did! Sold me last smile on Tuesday. Now I've nothing left to sell but me frowns!"

Tabetha handed the jar back. "No thank you," she said, as politely as possible. "I'm really not sure what I'd do with them."

With the jar cradled against his chest, the merchant looked left, and then right, as though to make certain no one else was watching. He leaned down close to Tabetha and cupped a hand to her ear, whispering, "A gift, Your Majesty. You never know when you'll need one!"

Tabetha felt the weight of something dropped into her pajama pocket. She watched the bald head of the frown-merchant disappear into the crowd, and then she glanced down to discover a small jar had been deposited into her pocket.

Great, she thought, lifting the jar for inspection once again. *What am I supposed to do with a bunch of frowns?* Tabetha was the empress of this land, after all, and frowning upon her subjects just wouldn't do. Which reminded her: That man had called her *Your Majesty.* In her blue pajamas and hospital slippers, how did he know Tabetha was the Empress of Wrush? Instinctively, her hands went to her head, then bounced away as if poked. Her crown was there. She was wearing it, a wreath of white petals sewn from orchids everlasting.

The crowds grew so thick that people pressed shoulder to shoulder. The melodic chirping of their lice filled the air. Tabetha saw tattooed leopards on leashes and magic carpets for sale. She saw ice-torches and jewelry and jugglers. Somehow, in the midst of all this commotion, she needed to find her friends. She looked around, exploring sights and sounds like she had never imagined. Her bed was on wheels, but she couldn't roll it alone. Until the Mungling came along with his saddle, as he usually did, Tabetha was pretty well stuck here in the market, hoping someone she knew might find her.

"A morsel, Your Majesty? A taste from my cart?"

A little man with a face like a camel pressed his way through the crowd. He pushed a squeaky little cart hung with bells. In big red letters across the side, his cart read: "Riddle Chef's Pantry." Then in smaller letters beneath it: "Baked Goods And Not Galore."

Tabetha realized his cart was nothing but a tiny wood-fired oven on rickety wheels. The camel-faced man opened the oven door and removed what looked like a fluffy loaf of bread. Tabetha loved fresh bread, and this smelled like the finest. Her stomach rumbled, asking in that strange language of churgles and pops if perhaps one slice of that loaf might be shared.

"That looks very tasty," she said, then looked down, patting each of her pajama pockets. "But I don't I have any money. If it's not too much trouble, maybe you could spare just an end piece or two?"

The little man lifted his chin. "Not to worry Your Majesty, I can give quite a deal. But from the back of your foot I'll require one heel."

"The heel of my foot?" She gaped at him. "For a heel of bread? What kind of trade is that?"

The man waved both hands before him as if to fend off her misunderstanding. "No, no, no, Your Dear Majesty, you make me sound like a crook! Not bread by itself, bread with butter and guk!"

Tabetha paused. "But I don't like guk."

The camel-faced man began digging around in an oven drawer, clanking and scraping through his pans. He turned back to Tabetha, face beaming, holding out a bowl of something thick and green, something that could well have been butter, once, but now jiggled like a bowl of snot as he pushed it toward her.

"Oh! Oh, thanks, yeah, but that one's probably your favorite. Actually I was just hoping for a slice of toast." Tabetha cleared her throat. "By itself, I mean. Without the butter."

"Absurd!" the man cried. "I'll hear nothing of it!" His eyes grew big and shiny. "Just as the dead of the night is not truly dead, then toast without butter is simply burnt bread! Nor is this just any old butter, this stuff is the best! It's mixed fresh with my toe jam to give it that zest!"

Tabetha smiled politely, swallowing back a funny taste in her mouth. "Well actually," she said, "I'm not even hungry."

"But you said you were!"

"I'm not."

"Unbelievable! How can this be?"

"Um."

"Not even for sweat-pops?" he went on. "Or a little deep-fried goo?"

Something jumped in her gut, and Tabetha's cheeks puffed out. "That's all very tempting, you see . . ." She brought two fingers to her mouth. "But I think I was just thirsty all along. If I look around here somewhere I'm sure I can find some water or something."

The little man grew more excited than ever, lifting a battered kettle in his shaking hands. "Why, there's no need, Your Dear Majesty, I've some hawk-feather tea! Second only to wings if you wish to feel free. I must warn you, however, like a bird with clawed feet, you'll peck at your food and stand on it while you eat!"

Tabetha felt a hand on her shoulder. "Come away from him, Your Majesty." Then a second voice piped up from behind, "I'm afraid this man's food will only confuse you."

Tabetha glanced up to find two faces peering down at her, both of them identical. Neither of them human. Indeed, no two stranger strangers have ever hovered above the siderails of a little girl's bed, for they can best be described as a pair of rooster-headed men in royal blue capes. They were very tall, and very skinny, with colorful feathers and orange beaks. They wore knee-high black boots, matching blue coats, and enough jewelry to decorate a Christmas tree.

"Who are you?" asked Tabetha.

"Shall we?" the first rooster asked the second.

"We shall." Without another word, they each grabbed hold of a bedpost and began wheeling Tabetha, bed and all, through the winding lanes of the Hubbub Bazaar.

"Your pardon please! Imperial business coming through!" they yelled as they pushed her bed. The crowds parted and bowed as Tabetha passed. She held on tight, for the roosters pushed rather quickly and paid little notice to the bumps.

"Where are you taking me?" she asked. "I need to find the Mungling, and get to the first pyramid."

"Not today, Your Majesty. Your pardon please! Coming through!"

Tabetha grabbed the bedrails as they thumped over a particularly bad stretch of road. Her voice bounced with the bed when she spoke. "What is going on? I don't understand what's happening!"

The rooster on her left answered in a prim voice. "By imperial order of Her Majesty, Empress Tabetha Bright the First, we have been summoned to take you directly to the Tower of Mrill without impediment, delay, stoppage, distraction or further intercolluptation." He cleared his throat before finishing. "Ahem. Not even if Her Majesty needs a towel to dry her face in the event of a water catastrophe."

"A water catastrophe? The Tower of Mrill? That makes no sense," she cried. "I *am* Tabetha Bright. I'm the empress, right here in this bed."

"Indeed." The rooster slowed not at all, thrusting a scroll in her face.

Tabetha opened the scroll only to gape at the handwriting. She recognized it as her own.

"What?" she mumbled. "I don't remember writing any of this." She scanned down to the middle, surprised as ever, and read the following:

' . . .*but do not, under any circumstances, stop for any reason.*
You must bring me, the Empress Tabetha Bright, to the Tower
of Mrill without delay. Even if I need a towel."

To Tabetha's amazement, the bottom of the scroll was signed by her hand, in the ink of her magic pen. Her fingers drifted down the page to touch her name.

"*-Tabetha Bright*"

"This is impossible!" Tabetha exclaimed. "How could I have written this if I only just arrived? Where did you get this scroll?"

She squinted at the page, reading it all again.

"And what's all this about a towel?"

Just then, Tabetha gasped in surprise as an apron of cold water splashed up and over the foot of her bed. She was drenched from head to toe, the roosters having bowled her bed right through an enormous mud puddle. Water trickled into her eyes and she wiped it away. She turned to look up at the roosters. Their faces were expressionless, though covered in mud.

"Uh, excuse me," said Tabetha. "I seem to have gotten a little wet with that last one. Would either of you happen to have a—"

"A towel?" The rooster tapped briskly at the scroll in her hand. "Empress' orders," he said. "No towel. No stopping. Pardon me! Step aside please!"

"But I *am* the empress," Tabetha insisted. "Don't you see? It's me who wrote these orders." Then she muttered, "Though I don't really see how that's possible. And I do wonder how I knew I would need a towel when I wrote them, as there seems no way I could have known about the puddle."

"Did you just say 'Trodad'?" one of the roosters interrupted. He leaned down close, suddenly interested.

"No," said Tabetha. "I didn't."

"Oh," said the rooster, and then added a few steps later, "because I thought you did."

Tabetha glanced uncertainly at her guides. They said nothing for a time and Tabetha coasted along in her bed, more or less forgetting the strange interruption when at last the same rooster said to her, "Because if you did, I was going to ask where."

"Where what?"

"Where I could find one, Your Majesty."

"One what?" she asked.

"A Trodad."

Tabetha wrinkled her nose. "You mean it's a thing?"

"Not a *thing*, Your Majesty. Surely you don't mean to offend them."

"Them?" she asked.

The rooster nodded. "The Trodads."

Tabetha thought for a long while, wondering which of her thousand questions would be best to ask first. She decided upon the simplest. "It may seem obvious to someone like yourself," she said, "but I don't know what a Trodad is."

"A Trodad?" The rooster appeared startled, as though she'd asked out of the blue. After a moment's consideration, he said, "Why, at first glance they look just like an *idea*. In fact, line the two up, side-by-side and you'll have quite a time trying to tell them apart. Except that a Trodad is generally pink in color— occasionally mauve— and when it puffs up its throat you'd do well to stand back, for it's likely to explode or sneeze lightning."

"I'm having trouble picturing this creature."

The rooster carried on as if she'd never spoken, " . . . was the first time I had the pleasure of seeing one. But apart from these habits, it's their language that separates a true Trodad from lesser creatures like opinions and afterthoughts. Beautiful language they have. Truly it is."

"Can you give me an example?" asked Tabetha. "Before just now, I'd never even heard of Trodads, let alone heard one speak."

"Certainly Your Majesty. Let's begin with your name. Do you know how you would say 'Tabetha Bright' in Trodad?"

"No."

"*Trodad*," he said.

"Oh."

"And do you know," he continued, "what the polite thing for one Trodad to say to another after sharing a fine meal and a wee bit of coffee in the sun?"

"No."

"*Trodad*," he said.

"Oh."

"But guess, Your Majesty, which king their favorite sport is named after? The game played with lawnmowers and porpoises?"

Tabetha frowned. "I think I can guess."

"So you see, Your Majesty, there really is no reason to be frightened."

"Was I? I think I'm sort of confused."

"Very well," replied the rooster. "I'm sure the Password Plants will gladly see you now."

By this point in her day, Tabetha was growing somewhat accustomed to such weirdness and peculiarity. She decided it best to expect the unexpected. She had managed to write her way back into Wrush with her magic pen, but her welcome could not have been more puzzling. If she could just find the Mungling, or better still the wizard named Answer, certainly they could help straighten all this out.

For now, however, Tabetha trundled along in her bed, not at all sure what was happening. At the mouth of an alley she passed a troupe of dancing dwarfs. They trumpeted away on nose-horns and pounded tortoiseshell drums. Elsewhere she saw smoke-sculptures and fuzz-merchants and salt-puppets on strings. *At least I'm in Etherios*, she thought, watching some low-flying clouds drift over rooftops and castles. *At least I'm here, where there's still hope of stopping Thomas Morlac.*

Upon the horizon, not far off, a lone silver tower came into view. From this distance it appeared straight as an arrow and nearly as slender, but so tall its summit was lost among the fluffy bulk of clouds.

"The Tower of Mrill, Your Majesty," said one of the roosters, dipping his feathery head. "Just as the empress commanded."

Tabetha started to argue, then changed her mind. It was no use. She had no idea how she could have written the scroll, or why she would be sending herself to the Tower of Mrill.

Yet here she was.

Tabetha found herself parked before the arched wooden door of the tower's entrance. The strange thing was, up close the tower was even narrower than it was from a distance. Tabetha thought three people standing inside, shoulder to shoulder, would feel quite cramped, and certainly there was no room for a stairwell.

"Is there a ladder or something inside?" she asked.

Just then, two long green vines slithered around from the back of the tower, each from opposite sides. They met together and twined before the door as though guarding it. Their heads, which had no eyes, were like the enormous buds of unopened flowers, and they whispered to each other like twins with a secret.

"Ahem," said one of the roosters. "Her Majesty, the Empress Tabetha Bright the First, now sits before the Tower of Mrill." He took the scroll from Tabetha and opened it up for the vines to read. "As you can see," the rooster told the vines, "Her Majesty has personally requested this visit."

The vines twisted around to face Tabetha. One of them poked out its bud-like head and hissed, "*Password.*"

"Password?" repeated Tabetha.

The two vines flinched in surprise, then whispered quietly to each other.

After a moment, the second vine hissed suspiciously, "Are you saying 'password' is the password?"

Tabetha glanced up the full height of the tower, this rod impaling the sky, then back down at the vines. "I don't really know. Is it?"

The vines gasped and sputtered. "Which are you saying? You must be more clear. Is the password 'password', or 'I don't really know?'"

"I mean I don't know what the password is."

"Ahk!" The vines jerked back as though burned. Tabetha watched them murmur together, occasionally peeking in her direction.

Such strange creatures, she thought. *If only they would stop listening to my words and just hear what I'm saying.* After a moment, the vines nodded to each other and one of them slithered forward. He coiled once around Tabetha's shoulders like a green scarf and whispered into her ear, "If the empress of Wrush doesn't know the password, then who does?"

Tabetha had no idea. "Are you saying you don't know either?" she asked.

"Of course not!" the vine snapped. "Do you think we would bother with you if we did?" The two vines withdrew in a huff and slithered back up the tower. Tabetha sat speechless atop her bed.

"Password Plants, Your Majesty," one of the roosters explained. "Entirely useless creatures, if you ask me, though they can speak nonsense fluently in over one hundred languages I'm told. Come along now, hup, hup. According to Her Majesty's orders, we are to have you atop this tower in . . ." He removed a gold pocket watch from within his blue coat and glanced at it. "Precisely four minutes, and not a second later."

Tabetha looked up at her guides. Never, in all her short life, had she felt smaller and more alone, more helplessly inexperienced in a baffling world as she did right then, with their rooster-cold eyes peering down at her.

"Are you trying to trick me?" she asked. "Because I can't always tell by people's faces. And I don't like it when people trick me."

"There is no trick, Your Majesty, simply following the empress's orders."

"But I *am* the empress, I've told you," she said. "I don't give anybody orders because I'm not very good at them yet. I don't know where you got that scroll, or how I might have written it. Mostly I don't know anything. Why can't you just help me?"

The roosters leaned in from either side, as if about to explain at last.

"Shall we?" the first rooster asked the other.

The second rooster nodded. "We shall."

Without another word, they hoisted Tabetha from her bed and carried her into the Tower of Mrill.

Splat.

$\mathcal{N}$ow it is a fact well known in the empire of Wrush that the Red-Breasted Mrill, a migratory bird, will lay its eggs only in a nest woven from the filthiest black hair. Not twigs and string. Not laces and lint. Black hair, and only the filthiest will do. Thus, the brightly-colored Mrill collects what it needs from the sweaty backsides of trolls as they sleep in dank caves, and it is for this reason the Mrill's nest remains safe from predators. You see, no creature in Wrush would dare approach such a nest, stinking as it does of trolls' grime, and though the Mrill doesn't know it, the word for its little ploy is *deception*. Yes, deception, the art of hiding one thing within another. And it is for this clever little bird, a master of the art, that the Tower of Mrill is named.

Gazing around the towers interior, Tabetha was astounded, to say the least. Of all the unbelievable things she'd seen this morning, nothing came close to what she found among the tower's inner chambers. "This is amazing," she whispered softly to herself, her wide eyes roaming from one wall to the next.

The Tower of Mrill, barely thicker than a tree from the outside, was vast as a palace within. White-tiled floors sparkled beneath great chandeliers. Marble pillars shone in the rich light. Gem-encrusted archways gave way to corridors and ballrooms, theaters and ice rinks. The winding stairwell could have hosted parades.

"How does all this fit inside such a skinny tower?" Tabetha asked, trying to keep the astonishment from her voice. There was something haunting about the quiet, about the brightness of it all. Her heart felt flooded with magic.

"I'm afraid I don't understand the question," replied a rooster as the pair carried her up the spiraling stairs. When they reached the second floor of the tower she asked them to stop.

"Sorry, Your Majesty. You are to be atop this tower in exactly three minutes. The empress's orders, you understand. Can't be late."

"But I want to look around," Tabetha argued, for the second floor was so grand it made the first floor appear plain. "I really don't understand what the rush is."

The roosters carried her up floor after floor, winding higher and higher around the staircase. Strangely, each window opened onto a new landscape: desert, jungle, starry nights over mountains, and underground cities. Twenty stories up, Tabetha peered out a window and found she was at the bottom of the sea. Through the window on the very next level she discovered a circus under way. On the level above that, a banquet. At some point, Tabetha peered over the edge of the railing. The bottom was so far below she felt dizzy. "How much longer till we're there?" she asked.

The rooster checked his golden pocket watch. "Precisely thirty-seven seconds, Your Majesty."

The stairs led straight up to the ceiling, upon which Tabetha saw a wide wooden door, a very large framed-painting of two yellow sailboats at port, and a window that opened onto the sea. The angle of it all was impossible, of course, but the roosters paid no mind. With Tabetha in hand, they carried her straight up to the door in the ceiling, and though she did not experience a shift of any kind, the door was suddenly not above her, but before her. Together the three stepped through.

Before Tabetha and her escorts lay an enormous desert. It stretched like an ocean of sand in every direction. A breeze swept her face, blowing wisps of hair across her eyes. "What happens in thirty-seven seconds?" Tabetha asked above the hiss of the wind.

"Twenty seconds, actually, Your Majesty, and I do not know the answer. I should think the empress does, however, as she instructed us to bring you here."

For the hundredth time, Tabetha exclaimed. "I *am* the empress!"

One of the roosters peered down at her. "Of course you are," he said, and then they all halted atop a single dune which over-looked the desert to the horizon. Tabetha found a large, very plump, red velvet cushion awaiting her atop the dune, along with a bright red umbrella of the same material. The roosters set her down upon the cushion, placed the umbrella in her hand, and without another word, they trailed off, one behind the other, into the desert.

Tabetha called after them, "What happens in twenty seconds?"

Without turning around, the lead rooster removed his golden pocket-watch and held it up to the light. In a voice faint with distance, he called out, "Five seconds, Your Majesty!" Then the roosters disappeared beyond the next dune, leaving Tabetha alone and stranded atop a red pillow in the desert, confused as ever, frustrated, very anxious, and entirely unsure what to do next.

"Please don't go!" she called after them, a sudden panic clutching her chest. "I don't know what I'm supposed to do here! I can't walk, and none of this makes any—"

Suddenly, Tabetha heard a hissing sound from above. She tipped back her velvet umbrella and peered up at the sky.

Splat.

Tabetha gazed down into her lap. Something soft and cool and red had landed there and Tabetha stared for a long, long time before picking it up, as surprised as she would ever be in all her life. Carefully, experiencing something between wonder and fright, she set the creature atop her palm and lifted it for inspection.

"Did you fall from the sky?" Tabetha asked it, then searched above for understanding.

But the little red salamander said nothing. It simply stared at Tabetha with its big glowing eyes while she sat wondering, just as you must be too, if there could be anything more peculiar than her first morning back in the magical empire of Wrush.

$\mathcal{C}_\iota$

"Ahoy there!" cried a voice. Tabetha turned. In the distance, she saw a bizarre creature galloping toward her across the desert. It was the Mungling! And he was wearing her saddle! Like all sun-wyrms, the Mungling had six legs, an enormous grin, and a body that glowed with otherworldly light. All in all, he looked like a giant caterpillar, roughly the same size as Tabetha, and among all the wonderful people and creatures Tabetha had come to know in Wrush, the Mungling was her closest friend.

"So good to see you, Tabetha! So perfectly, wonderfully good!" the Mungling cried, skidding to a halt before her and panting like a dog in the shade. "I came as fast as I could, you know." The Mungling embraced her, and then withdrew to give her a good once over. "You look terrific! A little rumpled perhaps, but no worse for wear. Nothing a new pair of pajamas wouldn't cure."

Tabetha could not have been happier to see anyone. "Oh! I'm so glad you found me," she began. "I only just got here, and already I've got more questions than leaves on a tree. Starting with this." Tabetha lifted her palm, bringing the little red salamander into plain sight.

"Bells and pumpkins! Is that for real?" The Mungling drew closer, curiosity plain on his puffy face.

"Look at that, he's smiling," said Tabetha. "I think he likes you." She tilted the red creature into one of the Mungling's six hands.

"I guess he does," chuckled the Mungling, bringing the salamander close to his eyes. "Hey there, little guy! Have you got a name?" To Tabetha he said, "Supposedly salamanders are rare here in Wrush, among the most enchanted creatures in all the empire, but I've never—"

And then it happened, so suddenly that Tabetha nearly bounced from her skin. A sound erupted, both soft and fierce, like the ghostly *whuuump* of a barbeque as all the coals catch fire at once.

And it came from the little red salamander.

With a brilliant flash, the salamander ignited, bursting into a ball of writhing, howling flame. The Mungling squealed like a girl pinched in the dark and then tossed the blazing creature in alarm.

It landed, cool as ever, in the hollow of Tabetha's lap. She stared in wonder. When her heart finally slowed, she offered a reluctant hand and the little red salamander wiggled aboard. Its skin was moist and cool, no sign at all of the flames. It looked up, slowly blinking its huge eyes, and Tabetha could only blink back at this tiny, innocent amphibian in her hand, a creature so red in color it needed a new word to describe it.

"Well, that was unexpected," said the Mungling as he wiped his damp brow. "Great little pet you've got there, Tabetha. Where did it follow you home from, the pits of hell?"

"He just fell into my lap," Tabetha explained. "The roosters set me right here on this big pillow and next thing I knew . . . *plop*! It couldn't have happened more perfectly. If I'd arrived a moment later he would have been injured." Tabetha petted the salamander and then slipped him into a second pocket in her pajamas. Upon putting him away, she was left with an overwhelming impression of power. The salamander's power. Almost— and it was strange to say— but almost as if she had just put a bit of the pyramid in her pocket, and carried it with her already. "Finding him just adds to my questions though," she thought aloud, "and I'd give just about anything for a single answer."

As if summoned by those words, a flash of gold streaked through the air, chirping like a flock of sparrows. "Answer!" she cried. "It's Answer's tattoos!" Then she pointed to the golden symbols swooping and flapping between her and the Mungling.

"He must have sent his tattoos to find you," exclaimed the Mungling. It was just like the boy-wizard to greet his empress in high style. Increasing in speed, his tattoos blurred into glittering ribbons, spiraling around Tabetha and the Mungling like a snake of light before zipping off toward the door in the desert.

"Come on! They want us to follow!" The Mungling helped Tabetha into his saddle, strapped her in tight and then raced through the door and back down into the Tower of Mrill.

C

The Mungling hurried Tabetha down flight after flight of stairs, at last bursting out the tower's front door into the blue of sunlight. "There!" he said, pointing to a flash in the distance. "His tattoos are headed straight for the Bubble Gardens!"

The Mungling galloped as fast as he could and Tabetha struggled to hold on. "We're losing them!" she shouted, but the Mungling just shook his plum-soft head. That's when she noticed the Pyramid Map etched there; mountains and rivers and dotted lines with strange writing, all drawn across the folds of his skin. On Tabetha's last journey to Wrush, she had discovered an image of the Pyramid Map floating on the surface of a pool. She copied the image onto paper, using the back of the Mungling's head for support. But the magic ink leaked through the paper and left a duplicate upon the Mungling's head. Soon after, Thomas Morlac took the original copy of the map, and this duplicate on the Mungling's head was the only one Tabetha now had.

She leaned forward in her saddle, calling into the Mungling's ear, "We should really make another copy of this map before it fades away! Only Morlac has another!"

"We've tried!" the Mungling called back, watching the tattoos' blurred tail turn a corner up ahead. "Each time, though, the copies we make just fade away, leaving the paper as blank as it started. I think it's because you drew the map with your magic ink to begin with."

The tattoos zipped beneath an arching gate and were lost from sight in the tall trees beyond. The Mungling followed, rushing under the arch and then stopping in the lush growth of an ancient garden.

"Where did they go?" Tabetha asked, searching the trees of the garden for any sign of Answer's tattoos. Everywhere she looked, strange plants curled or sung softly as she passed. Bushes of blue flowers shook with belly-laughter.

"This way, I believe," said the Mungling, leading her down a narrow trail through the garden. "If I know Answer, he'll be at the fountain, hard at work with his bubbles."

"I hope we find him soon," replied Tabetha. "Because we've got to be on our way. Morlac is searching for the first pyramid as we speak. It would be horrible if he got there before us."

Just then, the path opened onto a small clearing, a perfect circle of shorn grass surrounded by a dense wall of trees. In the center of it all floated a fountain. More like a bubbling birdbath, Tabetha decided upon closer inspection, and there beside it stood Answer. He looked up from the water.

"You've caught me at the perfect time, Tabetha," he said with a grin, then came forward to greet her. Answer's skin was dark and smooth, and his head was shaved clean. His tattoos, which had returned to his skin, appeared to be lit from beneath. They formed an unbroken line of golden symbols moving up one arm, across his bare chest, and then flowing down the opposite arm. Though he appeared to be about twelve years old, Tabetha knew he was in fact more than eight hundred. Answer wore only an old pair of knee-length leather trousers, shiny with wear, and his feet were bare as a sailor's. He was a regular rapscallion by the look of him, but Answer, High Wizard of Wrush, radiated such ease with himself as to make kings feel self-conscious in their finery.

When he began to bow, Tabetha lifted him by the hand. She

kissed him on the cheek and was immediately overcome by that unique warmth, that sensation of safety that always surrounded his presence.

"I've so much to tell you, Answer! Things you wouldn't believe! And Thomas Morlac is already headed for the Three Pyramids!" She paused, gazing around. "But what are you doing here, and why is it so silent by the fountain? I feel as though I've dropped into a dream."

"Not surprising," the boy-wizard replied. "Most people feel that way their first time here."

Tabetha peered through the trees. Nothing in the forest moved, as if it were frozen in a picture. The only sound was the soft churgling of the fountain. "Where exactly is 'here'?" she asked.

"The Bubble Gardens," he said, and his dark eyes twinkled with delight. "The closest thing we wizards have to a post office." He stepped to the fountain, which was a shallow stone dish of blue water, hovering magically in the air. The water's surface rolled and simmered as though bubbling up from beneath.

Answer removed a simple golden ring from one finger, and dipped it into the blue waters of the fountain. When he pulled the ring out, a tiny window of liquid was drawn across it, just as if it had been dunked into soapy water. He put the ring to his lips and blew. Out came an enormous bubble. It was iridescent in the light, at least the size of a melon, and clung neatly to the ring Answer held.

He whispered into it.

As the wizard spoke through the hole in the ring, Tabetha saw something like smoke fill the inside of the bubble. She thought she saw images too, but couldn't be sure. With a small clicking sound, the wizard kissed the gold ring. The bubble snapped free and floated up through the sky.

"That was beautiful," said Tabetha. "But I couldn't hear what you said."

He slipped the ring back on. "Magical words, mostly. Probably best you didn't hear. They would have been pure nonsense to your ears and made them itch like poison ivy. But I've sent other messages today that were not unlike proper letters. Look here! We have a response coming right now!"

Tabetha looked up, shielding her eyes from the sun, and glimpsed a second bubble descending from the sky. It fell like a ball in slow motion, and she chewed her lip in anticipation. She watched, holding her breath as it halted above the fountain. The bubble held perfectly still, as though gripped by unseen hands, then took on a glow like the moon, and popped.

A wet spray slapped Tabetha's face and she flinched in surprise, but it was the voice from the bubble that shocked her most. "*Greetings, Answer, High Wizard of Wrush.*" The voice was deep and strong and smelled rich as wood-smoke. "*I received your message,*" the bodiless voice continued, "*just moments before, and with the help of wizard Banthor here, I now hurry to send you my own.*"

Answer interrupted at that point, whispering, "It's Isaac, the captain of your guard, speaking now. I sent him a bubble just this morning."

The voice continued, "*. . . and though your report of our empress'* return is heartening, and the Pyramid Map remains in our care, my news is not nearly so comforting. I'm sorry to tell you, Answer, but the dark sorcerer Morlac has already taken our goal. He has reached the first pyramid. Its magic is his, and as soon as Morlac discovers the remaining two pyramids . . . the Hedge will be destroyed. The wall between worlds will come down."

Nobody spoke when the message finished. Tabetha closed her eyes in despair. "I don't understand," she said at last. "Thomas and I left for Wrush at nearly the same time. How did he get to the pyramid so quickly?"

Answer shook his head. "I don't know, Tabetha. I wish I did. It seems Morlac is stronger than we first imagined. I do know this, though. The Hedge is not yet doomed. Morlac will need all three pyramids to destroy it and until he does, the Pump Dragons won't be able to dig their Wink Holes to Earth."

But Tabetha was no longer listening. Her attention had turned to something in the garden, something she was certain wasn't there before. "What is that?" she asked, pointing to a pool of oil glistening in the grass. "I don't remember seeing it on the way in. Looks like it's seeping up through the dirt."

"Where?" asked the Mungling, headed right for it with Tabetha on his back.

"Right there!" she cried. "You're about to slip in—!"

The Mungling stepped straight into the oil. He scampered about, like a dog on ice, and then all six legs skated out from under him. Tabetha crashed to the grass with a thud, bumping her elbow but otherwise unhurt. Sticky oil glistened on her hands.

"Slicker than banana peels!" announced the Mungling as he helped Tabetha sit up, brushing off her back. She looked around, rubbing her elbow, then stopped in alarm.

Something was horribly wrong.

"Mungling," she started, then swallowed, feeling the muscles in her jaw go tight. She was in the same place; the garden was unchanged, the fountain still churgled like before . . .

"Mungling," she repeated softly. "Where did Answer go?"

"Oh dear," whispered the Mungling, looking closely at the strange oil for the first time. "I believe, little Tabetha, that you and I have just slipped in a Time Slick."

"Then to the World Bell, it is!"

I should point out that as people, we are unique among animals. This is true for precisely two reasons: First, whereas other creatures are rather quiet in their youth, gaining volume only as they grow, the young of our species are puzzlingly louder, right from the start, than the much larger adults who care for them.

A second, and more appalling difference is this: Of all the creatures big and small, hooved and hoofless, brainless and brained, only the human has completely garbled the meaning of time.

Not true for Munglings.

"This whole Time Slick business, it's really not so bad as you think," the sun-wyrm assured Tabetha, digging out an old rag from his saddlebag. "A nuisance, for sure, but this sort of thing happens all the time here in Wrush. People slipping backward a

[48]

day, or forward a week. I suppose you get used to it after a while. Always seems worse around August."

"How can people ever get used to a Time Slick?" asked Tabetha, watching the Mungling hum to himself as he wiped the oil from her slippers. If what he said was true, then she was now sitting in the exact same place, here in the Bubble Garden, but at a completely different time. A time when Answer was not in the garden.

"How is this even possible?" she asked, touching the smallest tip of her tongue to the back of her hand and then smacking her lips in disgust. The oil was bitter as aspirin, which she had once chewed by accident and, as everyone knows, is best swallowed whole. Fighting back the taste with thrusts of her tongue, she said, "Where I come from time pretty much goes straight, like in a line. At least I think it does."

"Ah!" said the Mungling, scrubbing at a splash on her neck. "But this is Wrush! Very different here, I'm afraid, very different. Back on Earth, time is what keeps all things past on one side of today, and all things coming on the other. Neat and tidy, right? Like a great calendar's gate, time is what keeps it all from trying to happen at once, you see, which would make one rather busy and spoils surprises. Not so, here in Wrush."

From previous journeys, Tabetha had learned that time moved slower here in Wrush, but what the Mungling now described sounded even more extraordinary. "What makes Wrush so different?" she asked.

"Wrush is *made* of time."

"Made of it?"

The Mungling nodded excitedly. "The whole world. Frozen time. Solid like a ball of ice." He thumped on the ground for emphasis. "Stays frozen too," he explained. "Except when summer sun heats up the crust and melts time a little bit, just enough to slick the surface here and there and wreak a general havoc with the goodfolk."

Tabetha stared at the oil gleaming on her hands, then the puddle in the grass. "So these weird little slicks are . . .?"

"Liquid time, Tabetha. Liquid time. Careful there." He took her by the wrist and began scrubbing harder than ever. "Looks like you've got too much on your hands. A recipe for trouble, mother Munglings always say. There you are now," he said, stepping back to examine Tabetha. "Good as new!"

She ran a hand up her arm. The skin was softer now, like a baby's belly, but the scent was not particularly pleasant. "This must be how Thomas Morlac got to the first pyramid so quickly," she said, absently tugging at the loose folds of skin at her elbow. "If he found a Time Slick too, then he could have gone back in time."

"Quite true, quite true," said the Mungling. "It's possible he has already spent days here in Wrush, searching for the pyramid, even if you both left Earth together."

Which made Tabetha think of her medicine, every day at noon. No way she planned to miss that. In what had become her habit here in Wrush, she set the alarm on her watch.

"There," she said, poking the buttons on the display. "Looks like I have about . . . twenty three Earth hours before I have to return for my medicine, and since time moves much slower here in Wrush, I probably have even more than that."

The Mungling nodded in agreement.

"I do wish we weren't alone, though," she said, dropping her hands to her sides. "I feel so much safer when the High Wizard of Wrush is near."

Splash!

Tabetha snorted in surprise as fresh oil spangled the air. She glanced at the Time Slick and found someone slipping and skidding around in the oil, trying hard, but failing to sit up.

"Answer!" she cried, recognizing the wizard's laughter.

"It took me a minute to figure out where you went," he explained as he struggled to his feet. "Then I realized you were right here, and the question to ask was not *where did she go to,* but *when.*"

"I should have known you'd follow," she said. "You always have."

"As I always will, Tabetha. I am your wizard, after all."

Tabetha bit her lip and drew a slow, thoughtful breath, suddenly filled to bursting with wonder. *How does it happen,* she asked herself, *that a lonely eight-year-old girl in a wheelchair ends up with a wizard of her own?*

Or a crown, for that matter. Or a Mungling or a throne, or any of the magic that made this world so special. In her struggle to save Wrush, and everything that went with it, Tabetha realized she'd rushed past all its beauty.

She sighed.

Like trampling the garden to get a view of one bloom.

Suddenly, Tabetha was reminded of this morning, sitting beside the window in her hospital room, trying to understand the nature of beauty. These questions, it now seemed, had been with her all day. But why? Was there something here she needed to figure out?

"Mungling," she said aloud, still thinking it all through. "Mungling, what is beauty? I mean . . . I know it's a waterfall, and a baby. And a song, and kind words, but . . . but what is it really? What is beauty really about?"

"You mean where does it come from?"

"Maybe," she said. "Or maybe I don't really know what I mean. It just seems like some things are beautiful, and some things aren't. You ever wonder about that?"

"I'm not sure," he confessed. "*Wondering* has never been a strong suit for us Munglings. We generally prefer to gallop!"

Tabetha smiled, lifting her gaze to the treetops which came to life in the breeze. "Did you ever see something so pretty you just ached inside? Like you could just crumple and cry from the beauty of it?"

"I don't know, Tabetha. It sure sounds nice, though."

"I dropped a quarter once, and it fell straight through a hole in a sidewalk grate," she said. "I lost it, and that quarter was all I had. I thought I would break down and cry right there, but then somebody I never met before crouched down in front of me, right there on the sidewalk, and gave me another one.

"It wasn't even the quarter that made me so happy," she went on. "It was a stranger stopping, for just one moment in their day, and doing something nice for another person. I can't explain it, but it made me feel something. Something so big inside I thought I might just laugh myself to smithereens."

Birdsong filled the silence when she paused.

"So it's like that?" asked the Mungling.

"So it's like that," she agreed.

"Then you do know what beauty is," said Answer. The wizard finished wiping off the oil and returned the rag to the Mungling's saddlebag. "You know what beauty is, Tabetha, because you just described it."

"I guess I do, when I feel it," she replied. "But how about when I don't? Since the moment I arrived here in Wrush I've been rushing around so fast, trying so hard to understand and to get to the pyramid and to help stop Morlac and all . . . I think I sort of forgot why. You know, why all this matters. And the answer is beauty, but I'm not really sure what that means anymore, or where we go to find it when it's lost."

"Can it get lost?" asked the wizard with a knowing grin.

"I don't know," said Tabetha. "Can it?"

The Mungling brought a fist to his chest and belched enormously before declaring, "Absolutely not. We Munglings are experts on losing every class of thing, yet try as we might, no Mungling has ever lost his beauty."

$\mathcal{C}$

Listen closely.

What I am about to tell you is true.

There was a time when I believed the toughest things in life, like death, a person endured only once. With age, I have come to see I was wrong. The toughest thing is joy, which comes and goes on a whim, if you are the sort of person who fears losing it.

Thomas Morlac was such a person. Tabetha was not.

Perhaps for this reason she, Answer, and the Mungling were able to set aside a brief moment, despite their great urgency, for the simple purpose of enjoyment, as the wise recognize such moments are golden. The three friends shared a small meal there on the grass of the Bubble Gardens, listening to the soft gurgle of the fountain while discussing their plans and otherwise soaking up the hurried goodness of the day. The Mungling had brought a whole assortment of treats in his saddlebag and they enjoyed a late breakfast of scrambled platypus eggs with a bit of coffee, followed by hunks of fresh black bread with jam and dolphin butter. Occasionally, Answer paused to translate the sweet twitter of birdsong into the epic poems each chickadee truly recited. Eventually, as indeed it was unavoidable, talk turned to the sorcerer Morlac.

Each worried the dark child would discover all three pyramids before Tabetha and gain the power to rip down the Hedge, which would be disastrous.

To rescue their golden moment, the Mungling suggested, "Let's forget that boy for a moment, shall we? The mere mention of Morlac' name puts a sour taste in my mouth, and right now I'm about as hungry as a pregnant Burbleglock."

Tabetha had no idea what a Burbleglock might be, or how much one might eat, but she knew from having spent a summer with her Aunt Bailey that if a pregnant woman didn't eat twice her body-weight each day, she became ferocious as a shrew—even downright dangerous if you were foolish enough to come between her appetite and the fridge.

"I have a question, though," she said as she set down her bread. Her legs ached, but she chose not to say so. "Has anyone stopped to wonder what day it is?"

The Mungling's face froze.

Answer blinked in astonishment. "Dear bells!" he burst out. "You're right! We don't even know if the Time Slick carried us forward or backward! Certainly this could change our plans."

"I believe it is yesterday," said the Mungling, lifting his nose to the air. "For the smell of horses is strong right now, as it always is the day before market. Caravans must be arriving from all around."

Tabetha leaned forward in excitement. "If it's yesterday," she said, "then we may still have a chance at the first pyramid! Thomas won't be there yet, and if we hurry we can catch him!"

"Do you think one day is enough time to find it?" asked the Mungling.

"Let's take a look at the Pyramid Map," said the wizard, gesturing for the Mungling to turn around. "That diagram on the back of your head should give us some idea of where we're headed."

Tabetha and the wizard now hunched close to the Mungling, inspecting the map together. She realized immediately that it was different from other maps she'd seen. When she looked closely at the rivers they appeared to be flowing. Clouds floated. Mountains sighed, and sometimes people, no bigger than vowels, scurried about among the lively stone-villages.

"What's this here?" she asked, pointing to a blotch of dark ink beneath the Mungling's left ear. "It looks like a lake, or maybe a town or something, but it's hard to tell without a name beneath it."

"Oh, actually that's an itch," replied the Mungling. "So sorry about that. I'm afraid I may have blurred a bit of the map before I remembered not to scratch."

The wizard traced his dark finger along a dotted line, a trail, climbing up and over the Mungling's folds of skin. "I don't think it matters," Answer said. "The place we need to go is still clearly marked. See here," he said, tapping the back of the Mungling's head. "The path to the first pyramid is plain as day."

Tabetha peered closer. "Then why is the end of that path marked with a bell instead of a pyramid?"

"Not just a bell," the boy-wizard replied. "A *World Bell*. According to this map the first pyramid isn't in Wrush at all."

"Then where?"

"Another world," said the wizard. "Which one, I can't yet say, but the World Bells were made to take us there."

"Like a Wink Hole?"

He nodded. "Only different."

"Then to the World Bell, it is!" came a deep voice through the trees. Tabetha turned to find Isaac, the captain of her guard, stepping into the clearing and she clapped her hands with glee.

"My Lady!" cried Isaac. "You're back!" The captain's blonde beard curled across his broad chest and he wore his blue tunic and a sword. He crouched low enough to look Tabetha in the eye.

"So good to see you, My Lady, and I'm proud to say the city has remained safe while you were away."

"No sign of Morlac?" she asked, thinking about the message Isaac would be sending tomorrow if she didn't act fast. "No news of him finding the pyramid?"

"Nothing, My Lady. If Morlac had found the first pyramid I would surely know by now. My spies are always on the watch."

Tabetha and Answer shared a knowing smile. *Then we really do have time*, she thought. Aloud she said, "By this time tomorrow, Thomas will have found the first pyramid. We have exactly one day to catch up and stop him."

Isaac's brows made a W in his confusion. "How could you know such a thing?" he asked, then turned to Answer who explained about the Time Slick, their most fortunate slip, and how they'd gained exactly one day in which to change things.

Isaac nodded sternly. "Then bring me with you, My Lady. You'll need all the help you can get, for surely there'll be trouble with Gwybies."

Instantly, their likeness came to mind— those terrible monsters with long claws and hooked fangs, a stench so foul they drew vultures. Any person with good sense, Tabetha knew, would do everything they could to avoid Morlac's Gwybies. She, however, would be racing straight towards them.

She shuddered at the thought. "I'd like you to come, too," Tabetha told her captain. "Which will make exactly four of us. You, me, Answer and the Mungling. Four against an army of monsters and a dark sorcerer's power." She drew a shaky breath, "I don't know if it's enough, but . . ."

"But it is what we have," said the captain. "And I will not leave you."

Tabetha stared. "You're not scared?"

Isaac went to one knee and took Tabetha's hand. It felt so tiny against his massive palm. He said, "Nobody fears Gwybies more than I, My Lady, for I have seen what they can do. The sight of their eyes alone makes me cringe."

"You sure don't seem scared. You never do."

"Oh, but I am, My Lady. I am. And yet it changes nothing." He smiled, and added. "Courage is not a heart without fear. It's a heart that moves forward and through it. Just as we've seen you do a hundred times before. You may not have the shoulders of a knight, or his skill with a sword, but your heart is the stuff knights are made of. It is why you were chosen to be empress above all others." He looked solemnly into her eyes. "And why I am forever sworn to protect you."

There was a moment of silence before the Mungling piped up. "A wizard, a knight, a Mungling, and an empress with a heart of gold. Sounds like a fearsome match if you ask me. Morlac might be wise give up now."

"We know he won't," said the wizard, lifting Tabetha into her saddle. "He won't wait around for us either. Come, it's time to leave. The World Bells are not far. We could be there by nightfall. After that, it's straight to the pyramid."

Answer strapped Tabetha into the saddle and fitted her feet to the stirrups. He straightened and paused, hands on his hips. "The only thing to worry about now is the Bellman."

"They've tricked us . . . They've tricked us all."

can almost see them now, so clear is this image in my mind, this image of Tabetha and her friends departing the floating city of Etherios. Can you see it too? It is a spectacular day, the sky flawless and bright with the domes of the city gleaming like white beetles. And there is Answer, like a small glowing orb beneath the glory of shadowless towers. Just behind him is the Mungling, humming with excitement, little Tabetha riding in the saddle upon his back. And in the front is brave Isaac, one hand upon the hilt of his sword, head swiveling left and right in search of danger. It is he who leads them through the narrow streets on this day, winding round alleys and over tanned-leather bridges, until they reach the soaring oak gates of the city's edge.

And beyond those gates, field upon field of white cloud.

It is easy, I am told, to forget that the floating city of Etherios is indeed floating high in the sky until one is presented with these heavenly views.

With the heavy wooden *clunk* of the gate at their backs, Tabetha and her friends left the scuffed cobblestones of the city behind and immediately sunk to their hips in pure cloud, high-stepping through it as if moving through snow-drifts. The Mungling licked his own shoulders as he walked, lapping up the sugary tufts. Tabetha reached down from her saddle and stroked cloud fiber as she would tangles of silk. They cleared downy hills and hiked fluffy ridges until Answer halted them at the cloud's ragged edge and flopped himself down, sinking into a scrumptious throne of dense cotton. "Now we wait," he said.

Looking out over the cloud's edge, Tabetha saw the ground pass slowly beneath. Boulders and trees, meandering streams. She cocked her head and found the Cloud Shepherd high above, smiling his great smile, his billowy flock of Cloud Sheep endlessly towing Etherios about.

In the near distance she saw mountains.

"Big ones," said the Mungling, pointing to their snow-capped shoulders and tipping his head back in search of their peaks. They were too high to be seen. "Do they have a top?"

Answer shook his head. "No one knows."

"Is that where we're headed, then?"

"Just beyond," the boy-wizard said, consulting the map once again. "To the Valley of Nether, where the ferns grow big as castles and are renowned for their mischief. Only the Bellman lives among them. Some say that's why he is the way he is."

"Who is this Bellman?" asked Tabetha, watching the mountains grow near. "Does he own the World Bells or something?"

"Or something," replied the wizard, pushing up from his spongy seat. "No one really knows where he came from, or how he does it, but the World Bells only chime for him. 'The Fern Slayer,' he calls himself. Crazy as a loon. Says he protects the bells from the forest." Answer climbed out to the edge of the cloud, pausing with one foot ahead of the other, as if preparing to leap. " Here we go, get ready."

"Are you crazy?" asked Isaac, clearly alarmed.

Tabetha gasped, her jaw hanging in awe. Barely five feet from their cloud passed the granite of a mountain. They drifted so near she could hear them. "They're . . . groaning," she said, and the wizard nodded.

"How else would one sing without a tongue?" With that, Answer flung himself from his cloudy perch and landed some feet away, clinging to the rocky rise of the passing mountain. "Come on!" he shouted.

Isaac shook his huge head in dismay, muttering, "Seems I have no choice." He leapt with a yell, landing in a steely clatter among the stones.

"My Lady!" he waved as Tabetha and the Mungling drifted past. "Hurry, before the cloud goes by!"

The Mungling worked his way to the very edge of the cloud, Tabetha clutching his saddle for dear life. The mountain had nearly passed them. To miss it would mean a thousand foot fall.

"Wait!" cried the wizard, for in that instant a ferocious wind had picked up. "Wait!" he called again.

"I'm waiting as fast as I can!" yelled the Mungling above the wind. But the mountain was almost passed. There wasn't a moment to lose. "Are you ready?" he asked Tabetha, scooting toward the edge.

"No! Not at—"

"Geronimo!" And he jumped with all the glee of young monkeys leaping from trees, crashing with laughter against the slope. He began to slide, Tabetha still fixed to his back, when Isaac threw out a huge hand and grabbed them. He hoisted them up without effort, congratulating the Mungling for his cheerful bravery while brushing them both off.

"These valleys are deep," Answer commented, looking down from his rocky perch into the lush forests far below. "None is deeper than the Valley of Nether."

Steamy mists clung to the faraway treetops; strange hoots and birdcalls bloomed up from below. "Looks like something prehistoric down there, like a place dinosaurs might live," said Tabetha to the Mungling, her gaze fanning the canopy.

"Dinosaurs? Pfff! No, nothing like that," he replied. "There are no dinosaurs this far south."

Of course, that there were dinosaurs at all came as a shock to the poor girl, but it was their absence, their absence from *here* that Tabetha found most alarming. After all, what place could be so terrible as to frighten away dinosaurs?

"Is it because of the Bellman?" she asked, her face growing warm with worry.

"It's because they're enchanted, these forests. They scare off all but the worst. Just wait till you see your first giant fern, Tabetha, and you'll see what I mean."

"What's so special about a fern?"

"Hey, look at that!" said the Mungling, pointing to her pajama pocket. Tabetha startled, finding the soft, blazing red head of her salamander peeking out.

"I almost forgot about him! Hey there little one. Are you hungry? What do these critters eat anyway?"

"Other critters, I imagine. Ask Answer, as he's just as likely to have asked a salamander himself, given his love for small things and their languages."

"I keep meaning to ask him," she said, "but there's just so much going on. And there he goes again, down the mountain. Will you remind me to ask Answer when we catch up? Or at least next chance we get?"

"Uh, certainly," said the Mungling with obvious hesitation. "Though I should say we Munglings are inclined to forget things ourselves from time to time. There is the one small issue of my name." He cleared his throat. "For example."

A name Tabetha knew he had forgotten. Her own promise to help him find it was still fresh in her mind, for she longed to see him return to his own nest in the sun.

"So if you'll just agree to remind *me*," continued the Mungling, "to remind *you*, well then, you'll be pretty well certain to remember whatever it is you and I are actually talking about right now, shall we go?"

Tabetha smiled and gave him a scratch behind the ear, and the two of them scampered down the slope after Answer and Isaac. They spent the remainder of the morning either sliding or skidding or in some mode of plunging, for the steepness of these mountains made walking impossible. The air grew warmer as they neared the bottom, steamy as a shower room, but it was the heady buzz of insects that struck Tabetha most of all.

There must have been millions of them, billions even. Like television static their sound rolled in her ears. Sometimes their pitch was near deafening. As Tabetha's group clambered down from the mountain into the jungle's dark depths, she thought she heard rhythms surfacing through their insectile song, pulses within pulses. She wondered if a person actually knew when she was hypnotized.

"How is the empress?" Isaac called from ahead as he dutifully slashed a path with his sword. Tabetha bumped along behind, up and down, up and down, holding loosely to the Mungling's reins and watching the forest with all the entranced fascination of a stargazer lying in a field.

Listening, always listening, to the insects.

"She looks a little pale," the boy-wizard called back. A moment later he added, "I'm no longer sure where we are. It's time we stopped for a breather."

The group gathered about the mossy rocks of a stream, where long looping vines dipped and danced on the surface. Nobody spoke much. Fingers of sunlight stretched down through the trees, and Answer seated Tabetha in a bright slash of it. The damp mosses steamed, dust twirled like galaxies, and strange beasts whooped in the distance. Tabetha lifted her chin to catch the sun on her cheeks.

Listening, always listening, to the insects.

"I don't understand it," she heard the wizard say, studying the back of the Mungling's head. "According to this map, we should have been there by now. In fact, we should have passed the World Bell at least twice already."

Isaac squatted atop a small boulder midstream, oiling his sword with black cloth. "Maybe it's gone. Or moved."

The Mungling shoved his face into the stream, slurping loud as a camel. When he finished, he wiped his wide mouth and took a seat on the moss beside Tabetha. "You seem a little quiet," he said, a thread of worry tightening his voice. "Everything all right?"

Tabetha's eyes were closed, her chin still tipped to the light. The insects had become an orchestra, a roaring symphony in her head.

"Tabetha?"

When the insects' shrieks came together, like notes in a song, Tabetha could almost hear words slip between. Not quite a voice, yet she understood all the same.

"Tabetha? Tabetha, answer me!"

But Tabetha didn't hear the Mungling. The insect's pulsing filled her mind, filled her limbs like sharp nectar.

"Answer! Come quickly! I think something's wrong with Tabetha!"

The song grew shrill. It grew loud and piercing. It screeched through her heart like train brakes. She opened her mouth to the forest. She tasted it.

"She won't answer me!" the Mungling cried. Someone shook her. "I can't get her to talk! Tabetha? Tabetha, are you all right?"

"They've tricked us," she murmured, and felt a tremor of shock run through her friends. Eyes still closed, she said again, "They've tricked us all."

Something brushed her arm and she heard the rustle of someone leaning close. Answer's voice was cautious when he spoke. "Who has? Tabetha, who has tricked us?"

She opened her eyes. "The insects."

And the buzzing shut off, sudden as a faucet. The silence that followed was a hiss in her ears. The sound of one leaf falling was like a thousand.

"The insects?" the wizard repeated, and Tabetha nodded, feeling as though an unseen bubble had popped in her mind.

"Their song," she said. "It had us walking in circles."

The wizard stood up, looking suspiciously about him. "They've stopped now, the insects. You must have broken their spell. I've read about such things before, insects that could weave a man's thoughts like yarn, but never did I suspect it could be so strong." He turned to Tabetha, a look of intense curiosity in his eyes. "How did you know?"

Tabetha shook her head, looked down. There was no way to explain. "Their beauty drew me in, I guess. I couldn't help it."

"Their beauty?" said the Mungling with a grin. "Have you figured it out then?"

"Figured what out?" she asked.

"What beauty is. Where it comes from, like you were saying."

"Oh," she let out a slow breath. "That." She tucked a strand of damp hair under her crown. "I don't think so. No more than before, anyway."

"Well, no doubt you will," the Mungling replied. "If anyone can figure it out, it's you, Tabetha. You proved that long ago. Tabetha? Are you okay?"

She had burst into a fit of coughing that felt like a small explosion in her chest. The Mungling scooted to her side and patted her back. Out of nowhere, it seemed, she was choking and wheezing. Her head felt hot, her limbs felt weak. It was a struggle just to catch her breath.

"It's okay," she squeezed out between coughs. "It happens . . ." she coughed, " . . . sometimes."

Isaac propped her up, his face pinched with concern. The Mungling fed her cool water from his palms.

"It's just my pneumonia," she said when the coughing receded and she took her first deep breath without pain.

"But you never did that before," argued the Mungling. "And you don't look too good now."

"I'm fine, really," she insisted. "It's just that lately it's like something grabs hold of my chest and . . . I feel better now, though. I'm just weak, that's all. Please don't worry. I'll be ready in a minute."

"We'll stay here for the night," Answer announced. "There's no way Tabetha can travel right now."

"No!' she cried, choking back one last surprise cough. "We have to keep on! Thomas will reach the pyramid before us!"

A tense moment followed, for everyone knew this was true.

"She's right," Isaac said at last, and all eyes turned to him. "As much as I hate to say it, the empress is right. We must keep on. Too much is at stake if we fail."

Answer touched her cheek. He seemed unwilling to agree. "She can't even sit upright. There's no way she can ride the Mungling."

"Then I'll carry her," said Isaac. "At least until she regains her strength. If the empress wishes it, that is."

"I do," she said without pause. "And you must. It's like you said, Isaac, 'Courage is not a heart without fear. It's a heart that moves forward and through it.' Too many people are counting on us. We have to keep going."

Answer sighed through his nose. "All right. But I don't like it at all. And if the empress gets worse, I'll insist we stop. I won't agree to this otherwise." His dark eyes glistened with concern, and his tattoos gleamed brighter. "Do you promise, Tabetha? Do you promise to stop if you feel worse?"

She wanted to. Her chest still burned and her legs were cramping. If she did get worse, how *could* she continue? It seemed nearly impossible already. Yet these things she kept secret, and she chose instead to say, "I'm sorry, Answer. I can't make that promise. I've already made another to myself."

"Ho there, Wind Rider! Ho!"

*F*irst thing we'll have to do is figure out where we are."
Answer padded silently through deep leaf mulch, occasionally
glancing up through the trees, trying to get a glimpse of those
mountains beyond. He was clearly troubled by Tabetha's decision, but would do all he could to see their task through.

"Can you see anything?" she asked from the cradle of Isaac's
massive arms. Her captain lumbered along behind Answer, the
Mungling trotting merrily at their side.

Answer shook his head. "The forest canopy is too dense here.
I can barely see sky, let alone recognize mountains by their
ragged scraps and patches." He halted. "Notice we haven't come
across a single giant fern? That's a problem. I think it's time we
try something else."

"Like what?"

Answer leapt, graceful as a cat, atop a nearby rotting log. He
sat and crossed his legs there beneath the soaring trees, his dark

skin drinking in the shade. Tabetha was struck by the beauty of him, how magnificent he looked, like some creature of the forest older than time itself, this magical boy with tattoos. He lifted a hand and beckoned them near.

"What we need right now is a bird's eye view," he said. "That's what you call it when a place is seen from above."

"Okay," said Tabetha. "So how do we do it? Can you fly or something?"

The wizard grinned at that. "No. But if one of us happened to have *a bird's eye* . . ." He leaned forward, reaching behind Tabetha's ear. When he withdrew his hand he held something like a shiny pebble between two fingers.

"What is that?" Tabetha asked. Everyone bent close.

"Why a bird's eye, of course. All empresses keep one or two on hand." He smiled, clearly delighted to share his magic with Tabetha.

Where it truly came from, Tabetha didn't know, but this pebble really did look like a bird's eye. It was polished black with a tiny red ring in the center.

"Care to see how it works?"

Tabetha nodded eagerly.

Answer popped it in his mouth. "Firth, you haffa warmatup," he muttered awkwardly around the pebble on his tongue, then opened Tabetha's little hand and spat it into her palm.

"Can you feel it?"

She nodded again. "It's cool," she said, then frowned. "And . . . *hot*."

"Look inside," he said. "There, just inside the red ring."

Tabetha stared into the magic bird's eye. Immediately, the red ring began to spin, the black center sucking her in. As though at the end of some fisherman's hook, she felt herself yanked free from her body and reeled into blackness, and the next thing she knew, Tabetha was high above, the wind whistling in her ears, gazing down upon deep-forested valleys. Looking into the bird's eye, she realized, allowed her to see all that a bird sees.

She glided over dense blankets of green, the occasional white tree in bloom. Mist slithered up the long valley and slept there. Then the glitter of sun revealed water below. A stream wove through the trees like silver thread. *There*, she thought. *That's where we are now.* Then she saw the faraway place they were headed.

Far up the valley, where the mountains pinched together, a lush woodland of enormous ferns crowded and twined. She focused her vision, as though through a pair of binoculars, and suddenly she was directly above them.

"Whoa," she murmured, gazing down into the fern forest below. Tremendous green fronds unrolled like carpets across the canopy. She saw every detail clear as day. Then, as abruptly as it all started, it was over. She was jerked back into her body like a rubber-band snapping.

Bird sounds.

The scratchy soft feel of moss against skin.

She opened her eyes and found herself sitting with the magic pebble in her palm. "I've seen it," she said aloud. "I've seen the Valley of Nether."

"We all have," said Answer, and the others nodded in

agreement. "The question is . . ." He retrieved his pebble and slipped it into a pouch. "Has it seen us?"

$\mathcal{R}_\ell$

"How could a forest see us?" Tabetha asked as they trekked east up the valley, the scent of wetness and mold growing thicker. "And does it even matter? It's not the forest but the World Bell we're looking for anyway."

Answer pushed aside a tangle of vines, then held back a branch so it wouldn't slap Tabetha as Isaac carried her past. "The magic of the bird's eye is tricky," he explained. "If we saw the Valley of Nether, it almost certainly saw us first. Nonetheless, to answer your question, *yes*. I think it does matter. I'd have preferred to have found the Bellman first, that way he could lead us through the ferns without harm."

"Ferns!" called the Mungling up ahead, bounding through foliage like a ridiculous deer. "They're huge!"

One by one, her friends passed underneath, each tipping their heads back in silent marvel. She felt about as tiny and insignificant as an ant in a meadow.

So this is a giant fern . . .

It climbed thick as a redwood through the dense forest canopy, its great fronds uncoiling overhead. The darkness of shade beneath was nearly complete and their footsteps made a muffled echo on the mulch.

"It's like midnight at noon down here," Tabetha commented. Fireflies winked like shooting stars through the air. Nothing else grew in the darkness. Not a plant, not a shrub. "I never imagined a fern forest would be quite so eerie."

No one replied, as if mistrustful of their own voices. They treaded on, cautious and quiet, and Tabetha thought she could even feel the darkness about her. It caressed her pale skin, soft as spring plumage. An unfamiliar scent reached her nose.

"Smell that?" she whispered. It was earthy and faintly sweet. And pungent, like black incense.

"Fern Shadow," the boy-wizard whispered back. "Potent stuff. Corked and bottled, it will suck the black out of night." He sniffed. "That smell tells us it's awake."

"I sort of like it." Tabetha stirred circles in the Fern Shadow, feeling the thick weight of it against her fingers.

"I wouldn't play with this darkness, Tabetha," the wizard warned. "Just as a man will cast shadows by light of the sun, here, in these parts, Fern Shadows cast *men*— or beasts—according to their class of mood." He walked on in silence for a bit. "I believe the Bellman may have been among the first of them."

Something wailed in the distance, and Tabetha clapped a hand to her mouth. Answer paused. "Tarantulope," he whispered. Then something— or perhaps many somethings, a spectral herd of countless hairy legs— bounded across the edge of Tabetha's vision and disappeared into the darkness beyond.

"They're gone now," Answer breathed. "More frightened of us probably." But Tabetha's breath would not slow, sounding loud as a saw against the ghostly silence of this place. Suddenly the darkness was not a game, but a thing of dread, hiding dangers she dare not meet.

"I don't like this forest anymore," she muttered to herself and Isaac patted her gently. These ferns were too big, this darkness too dark. Tabetha wanted to find this Fern Slayer, get to the World Bell and get out of here.

Not far ahead, Answer suddenly halted without a word. The Mungling caught up and paused beside him, both of them staring into the inky gloom as Isaac and Tabetha approached. She struggled for a view.

"What is it?" she murmured, trying to push herself up in Isaac's arms. "Is there something out there?"

"Shhhh," whispered the wizard. "I mean yes, but *shhhh*."

Nobody moved.

The earthy scent grew strong.

Far in the distance, a small light appeared. It bobbed up and down, growing brighter as it neared. Before long the light became a lantern.

"Who is it, can you tell?"

The lantern jounced at the end of a long stick, swaying side to side over bumps.

"It looks like a . . . a goat," said Answer in an astonished whisper. "A mountain goat. Carrying something very fat on its back."

Then a voice cried out from beneath the lantern's glow, "Ho there, Wind Rider! Ho!" And out of the darkness appeared a furry white billygoat, stumbling down the path with the oddest man atop its saddle.

Tabetha grinned, utterly puzzled by the sight. If the sudden appearance of a goat wasn't strange enough, the man astride it was sure to draw wonder. He was short, red-faced, fat as a barrel, and stiff at the joints with shiny armor at least two sizes too big. He would have reminded Tabetha of a plump sausage in tinfoil if it weren't for the absurdity of his hat— a car's hubcap, rather dented but polished, held snug to his head with a chinstrap. He carried a lantern pole in one hand and the goat's reins in the other. At his hip hung a long soupspoon like a sword.

"Ho, Wind Rider!" he called again and the furry goat brayed softly and halted. The fat little man leapt down from his mount with all the grace of a saucepan and lifted a pudgy hand in the air. "Friends!" he called, jangling loudly as he approached. "Welcome! Welcome to our forest! Please, do not be alarmed by my steed. He is fierce only in appearance. Come Wind Rider! Greet our new friends!"

At that, the man's little goat stumbled to his side, and Isaac whispered in Tabetha's ear, "This man calls his goat 'Wind Rider,' My Lady. He is not right in the head."

The little man carried on like an old friend, his voice somehow too big for his body. It was preposterously deep and loud, bringing to mind radio announcers and cartoon characters each time he spoke.

" . . . so few visitors to our perilous lands!" he was shouting, "But if you are in need of fine company, I can surely assist!"

"Actually," said Answer. "We seek a man."

"Which man?" The newcomer's eyes grew small and suspicious. The earthy scent grew thick.

"The Bellman," replied Isaac. "The one who calls himself the Fern Slayer."

The little man drew his wooden spoon like a weapon and

waved it threateningly in Isaac's face. "Who sent you? Hmm? Are you with *them*?"

Isaac stepped back, for he still held Tabetha in his arms. "'Them,' who? We've been sent by no one."

The little man cocked his head to the side. "Them." His chin indicated the ferns.

"We're looking for the World Bell," Tabetha quickly interrupted. "According to our map, it will take us to the first pyramid. We have to get there soon, or else an evil sorcerer will destroy its magic, and maybe even the Hedge. And if that happens, the Pump Dragons will finally dig Wink Holes to Earth in search of food, leaving a perfect path for Morlac's army of Gwybies to follow across." She paused, meeting his small eyes. "You're the man we're looking for, aren't you. You're the Bellman."

"I am the Fern Slayer, if that's what you mean." He held his long spoon upright, gazing lovingly upon its rounded tip. He drew an admiring finger down the length of it. "I call her 'Fernsbane.' A true wonder, hmm? There is no blade quite like her. Have you ever seen such craft?"

"No, never," replied Tabetha, finding she liked this little man for reasons she couldn't explain. "If you would be so kind, we need you to take us to the World Bell. We would go ourselves, but—"

"Hah!" The man sheathed his wooden spoon and turned on heavy heels, taking up his lantern pole and sputtering. "Come Wind Rider!" Tabetha watched him recede into the darkness, muttering to himself above the clanking of armor.

"I think we're meant to follow," she said.

Isaac whispered, "He is a madman, My Lady. I do not trust him."

"Trust!" the man hollered, without stopping or turning. "He says he does not trust, when it's the girl who keeps the secret of salamanders!"

Tabetha startled. "I almost forgot! I found a— but how did you know?" she called after him.

The Fern Slayer stomped ahead without answering, arguing loudly with himself or his goat. Tabetha removed the salamander from her pocket. She held it up in her palm.

It glowed.

Answer brought his face close, his dark eyes glistening in the salamander's light. "Dear bells," he whispered to himself in amazement. Then he looked to Tabetha. "Where did you find this?"

"I . . .I think it found me. In fact, I've been meaning to ask you. From the moment I arrived in Wrush I seemed to have been expected. I can't imagine how. I was taken to the top of the Tower of Mrill and placed just so in a desert. A moment later this salamander landed in my lap. As if it too were expected."

"I've never seen one quite like it." Answer seemed unable to pull his eyes from the creature. "Wrushic Salamanders are among the most magical of creatures. In some legends they are even called keys."

"A salamander key?" she chimed. "I never really thought of an animal like that. How can he be both a salamander and a key?"

The boy-wizard looked up, biting his lip before speaking. "Has it . . . Did it yet show you its heart?"

"I think so. But only once," said Tabetha. "When the Mungling picked it up, the salamander burst into flames like a fireball."

Answer nodded. "I have no idea why this creature has come to you, Tabetha, but you're fortunate. That much is clear. Very few people have ever handled one."

So you're a salamander key, Tabetha thought as she stroked him, then slipped the creature back into her pocket. "I feel a little better, Isaac. I think I can even ride. Please set me back on the Mungling."

He did so, and Tabetha started off after the lantern's soft glow, the Mungling chattering to himself as they went. "What do you think of the Bellman?" she asked him, but the Mungling was too caught up in some story or another to hear it. She pushed his voice aside, wondering about this Bellman instead, this strange fellow who smelled of Fern Shadow and seemed to know things he couldn't. Perhaps he had more to tell her. Like about beauty, and where it came from. She decided to ask him as soon as she caught up.

The Mungling's steps echoed beneath the high ceiling of ferns, though Answer and Isaac barely made a sound. When they finally reached the Bellman, he was sitting in the halo of his lantern atop a carved block of stone. It was part of a ruined staircase by the look of it. Other stone steps rose steeply behind him. Tabetha looked around, trying to see where they went, but nothing was visible beyond the lantern's glow.

"So where is this World Bell?" she asked him.

"Who is it that asks?"

Isaac stepped forward and barked, "This is the Empress of Wrush! You are her subject!"

The Bellman bit into a huge chunk of cheese. With his mouth full, he said, "I have no empress. I serve only the queen."

"The queen?" repeated Isaac. "There is no queen."

"Oh, but there is. She may be old and broken, but her voice is still sweet. You shall see. You shall hear her song. But first," he announced in that too-big voice. "First tell me this, little girl! What has a spine in its back but not one single bone? What can speak every language without hint of a tongue? Hmm? *Hmm?*" He stood up, but not very tall, wiped his mouth with the back of his hand, and tossed the remaining cheese over his shoulder.

"Um," Tabetha stuttered. "Uh . . . is it . . . a mountain? I mean no, no wait . . . the wind?"

"A *book!*" he yelled near the top of his lungs. "A book!" The Bellman shook his hand in the air with wild emotion and then thrust it beneath the armor of his breastplate. He fumbled around a moment, as though searching or scratching, then withdrew a small book and waved it in the space between them, demanding, "You see? You see?" Then he muttered under his breath, "'A mountain' she says . . . Hah! Next she'll be calling Wind Rider a goat and asking to ride my noble steed."

Pressing the book into Tabetha's hands, he announced, "Lesson number one is patience! *Patience!*"

"Thank you, I think," she said, studying the book. It had a dark leather cover, rounded slightly to the shape of his chest. Every page within it was blank. She flipped through the pages again, making sure she hadn't missed something. "Can I ask you what I'm meant to do with it?"

"Make yourself a note," he said, picking his teeth. "The most important one you'll ever write. Have it sent back to Etherios with specific instructions to be carried out upon your sudden appearance in the Hubbub Bazaar tomorrow. Begin like this:

On Friday, the 29th of August, two roosters are to be sent through the marketplace in search of myself. I will be found in my bed, not long after noon. I will be wearing pajamas. I will argue with you, and behave as though confused, but do not, under any circumstances, stop for any reason."

Tabetha put down her pen, these words suddenly familiar.

The Bellman continued, " . . .*You must bring me, the Empress Tabetha Bright, to the Tower of Mrill without delay. Even if I need a towel.*"

There was more of course, but Tabetha could not believe her ears. This was the very note she'd read earlier in the day, the orders the roosters had insisted she'd given! So this was how she had come to write it. She stared at the Bellman, thoughts racing through her head.

Since she'd slipped back a full day in the Time Slick, she realized, she could send this note now and it would reach Etherios tomorrow, just in time for her arrival from Earth in her bed. Tabetha looked down at her writing on the page, thinking how much it had confused her. In truth, these were not even her orders, but the Bellman's. This letter would instruct the roosters exactly where to take her, and when, in order to catch the salamander in her lap.

Which brought up the question of why? What was so important about this salamander? And what was he the key to?

She took him out again, his damp red skin clinging to her
own.

"Mr. Bellman," she began. "It seems you know all about my
salamander. Why is it I was supposed to catch him?"

The Bellman became suddenly distracted. He turned to the
forest, his armored back glinting in the lamplight. "How dare
you!" he raged at the darkness.

Tabetha looked around. "Who are you talking to?"

"He's mad!" exclaimed Isaac.

"You challenge *me*?" the little man yelled to no one, then
drew Fernsbane above his head and charged into the black,
swinging and thrusting until his grunts grew faint and then
disappeared altogether.

He was gone. Just like that, the Bellman had left them. A
moment of confused silence followed, whereupon the friends
avoided one another's eyes and wondered what to do next.

Isaac shifted nervously. "All the better, I say," he decided
aloud. "That fellow's spent too long in these woods. His mind's
cracked. It's gone on safari, as we say back home."

"Don't be so sure." Answer retrieved the completed note of
instructions from Tabetha, glancing down the page as he spoke.
"Things are not always what they seem when it comes to magic,
or magical creatures such as him. I suspect the Bellman and
these ferns are not two things, but one."

"He says he fights them."

"And he may," replied the wizard, looking up from the paper

to meet their eyes. "But Fern Shadow is as potent as any potion I know. I'm not saying I understand this Bellman, only to look deeper than the face of things."

Answer whistled magically between his teeth, and two of his golden tattoos lifted into the air, one from each arm. They hovered there like hummingbirds until he held up Tabetha's letter in one hand. They grabbed it at the corners and flew off into the dark.

"There we are. Your letter should reach you in time," Answer said to Tabetha. "Those two tattoos are among the swiftest I have."

He walked to the Bellman's lantern pole, which was wedged upright between two blocks of the stair. He tugged it free with both hands, then held it up like a fishing pole to bathe them all in its glow.

"Now to see about this queen of his."

"Only beauty knows beauty."

$\mathcal{I}$f you were to ask Tabetha how she felt in that moment, staring at the wizard upon a staircase of ruins, golden lamplight dancing in his eyes, she could only have said *mystified*. A word that means "deliciously bewildered." A word that makes your lower lip hang, sends sweet tingles up your spine, and brings to mind treasures that lay hidden in the mist . . .

Mystified.

It should unravel on your tongue.

"The queen?" Tabetha sputtered as Answer turned to climb the stairs. "You mean you know what the Bellman was talking about?"

She followed upon the Mungling's back. Answer held the lantern pole before him, and with each step he took the soft light revealed a small patch of their path. Tabetha could see only disconnected bits of their surroundings in the lantern's glow, but all together she thought it was a tower they climbed. A stone tower, ancient and crumbling.

"The Bellman may have mystified us," said Answer as he climbed, "but this queen of his has not. What would a Bellman be loyal to, if not a bell?"

"The World Bell," Tabetha whispered in realization. "The World Bell is his queen. You think it's somewhere in this tower? Maybe at the top?"

"I do," Answer called back. "So did Thomas Morlac and his Gwybies."

Tabetha frowned in confusion.

"Their tracks are everywhere about the base of this tower," Isaac explained. "This Bellman seems to have let Morlac through first."

A fresh panic clenched her heart. Morlac was ahead of her still! "Please, please let us get there first," she murmured aloud, then urged the Mungling to move faster up the tower's cracked stairs.

Isaac remained just behind them, ready to catch her if they fell. It was a treacherous climb. Some steps were missing, others overgrown with thick roots that lassoed old statues and clutched limestone blocks in their knots.

When they reached the top, they found Answer grinning in the lantern light, gliding one hand across an enormous iron bell. Its size surprised Tabetha. For some reason she had imagined it would be small, but the bell was bigger than a tipi. It hung suspended from a stone lintel so high off the ground that even Isaac could pass underneath.

Answer reached up and rapped it lightly with his knuckles.

"I believe we've found your World Bell, Tabetha." It was properly bell shaped, like an old ballroom dress, with a wicked crack crawling up one rusty side.

"How do you know for sure?" she asked.

"By the writing here." Answer pointed to an area of raised lettering along the bell's rim. "It reads in the Old Tongue, a language we no longer speak, but see here? It tells us to stand inside the bell, then mentions the word, *Tsepudra*."

"'Tsepudra?' What's that?"

"A place. A whole world, actually, almost as big as Wrush. And much, much older. Not nearly so nice as Wrush though, with its hideous bogs and poisonous fumes. Tsepudra's a perfect place to hide a treasure, come to think of it."

"Then that's where Morlac is," she said. "That's where we'll find the first pyramid and where we have to go." She glanced up at the World Bell. "But how are we going to work this thing without the Bellman?"

"Maybe he'll come back," said the Mungling.

"That fellow? I wouldn't count on it," said Isaac. "We'd be better off waiting for Morlac to pitch in and offer us a helping hand. But look at that." He pointed directly beneath the bell, where a rusty winch was fixed to the stone platform of the tower. It was clearly made to lift and lower the bell as needed. Isaac stepped beneath the bell and threw two mighty hands across the winch's lever. He struggled against it, the veins in his arms bulging blue. There was a groaning and a grinding until at last the lever broke free, and Isaac let out enough rope to make the bell creak.

"The bell is lowering!" Tabetha remarked, watching it descend slowly around Isaac like a tremendous iron helmet.

"Quickly! Get under!" Isaac called, his voice ringing hollow from inside.

They hurried under the bell's rim, which halted at the level of Answer's waist, and dropped no further.

"That's as low as it goes," Isaac declared, wiping the sweat from his upper lip. "What now?"

"We're to ring the World Bell," Answer explained. "As long as we're inside it, the magic of the chiming will carry us to another bell just like it, most likely in Tsepudra."

Like telephones, thought Tabetha.

She was set down on the floor while the others searched for a way to ring the bell from within. A rope, she heard someone say. They were looking for a rope to pull.

Tabetha marveled at the sound of her breath, how loud it echoed inside the iron dome above them. She peered out into the night beyond, for she alone sat low enough to see under the bell's rim. The lantern remained on its pole, and she could hear it fizzle, the shadows of its smoke writhing across the cool, stone floor. Farther out, in that place where light mixed with gloom, Tabetha noticed something hanging. A thick braid of rope, she realized, though it hung well beyond her reach. To tug its frayed end she would have to be well outside the bell, leaving her behind and alone when the bell rang. She pointed to the rope, thinking to tell her friends, when the voice of the Bellman spoke clearly in her mind.

"*One more thing, little girl . . .*" The shadows squeezed tight, and his face briefly appeared. "*Only beauty knows beauty.*"

He pulled on the rope.

The bell chimed like thunder.

Shadow swallowed all but the sound.

Tabetha never did figure out whether it was the magic of the chiming or the Bellman's last words, but two things happened in those final moments beneath the bell.

First, she heard every sound ever made, all at once, as if all had been coiled tight within the World Bell's chime. She couldn't explain it after, she only knew it was so.

Second, her body dissolved into that strange collective of sound the way sugar does in a glass of warm water. She became the music of the bell, and she went where it went.

It wasn't until Isaac began cranking the winch again, and the bell lifted high enough for everyone to see beyond, that Tabetha knew for certain she was someplace else; a place other than Wrush.

"Tsepudra," she heard the wizard whisper, followed by the distant pop of a volcano spewing fire. They were everywhere, it seemed, these angry mountains of flame. Their red summits glowed like cigar tips in the night. "I warned you it would be foul here," Answer continued. "Tsepudra is well known to be the ugliest of all worlds."

Was it a twist of fate, Tabetha wondered, that brought her to such a dreadful place when it was beauty she so dearly wished to discover and understand? And what had the Bellman meant when he'd spoken his last words?

Only beauty knows beauty . . .

Tabetha looked around her and wondered.

Everywhere she turned, a barren land glared back, a land of steaming lava and waste. The sky flashed red with each volcanic blast. In the momentary light, Tabetha saw flakes of grey ash raining down like a snowstorm.

Answer stepped from beneath the bell, the first to brave this new land. "There is no point in waiting. Daylight never comes to this world. If we are to find the pyramid then it is to be through this."

He swung his arm wide, gesturing to this wasteland that knew a hundred and one shades of black; where blasts of fire— the only intrusion of light— were quickly quenched by the all-devouring gloom.

The air was heavy and hot. It burned their noses just to breathe. The ash gathered in their hair like hot snowflakes. Tabetha reached into the wrong pajama pocket, mistakenly touching the jar of frowns, then found the salamander curled in the opposite pocket. It brought her some small comfort to feel its cool skin, knowing all else she touched would scald her. She asked herself, with a rush of anticipation, what role this little creature might play in an adventure that seemed near its end.

Not a small one. That much was clear.

Tabetha and her friends started out from the World Bell,

climbing down the ancient steps of a tower much like the one they had left behind. Except this tower was black. Polished black, with stones that gleamed red when the sky did. The statues along the steps were of demons and gargoyles with eyes of hateful black sapphire. Tabetha's group hurried from beneath their hideous gaze, taking the steps two at a time. Instead of relief, however, reaching the ground brought only a new kind of dread. The soil was etched and torn with footprints. Hundreds of them.

"Gwybies," Isaac spat, crouching among the prints. "And these tracks are fresh. Morlac and his creatures can't be far ahead."

A volcano exploded, shaking the ground like an earthquake. It vomited lava and ignited low clouds. In that brief moment of light, Tabetha gazed down from her saddle, noting the Pyramid Map on the back of the Mungling's head.

It had changed.

Looking closer, she could find no sign of Wrush at all. There was no Etherios. No Valley of Nether. Instead, all the map's markings were now those of this land. Tabetha looked closer and found the World Bell, which was now at their backs, as well as range after jagged range of volcanoes. A dotted line on the Map traveled through the Marshes of Krud. Beyond that Tabetha saw a triangle, which could only be the pyramid. "The Pits of Prantis," she muttered aloud, pressing her finger to the name beneath the triangle. "That must be where the pyramid is. The Pits of Prantis."

"It's this way!" she shouted beneath the trembling sky. "I've found the pyramid on the map, and it's this way!"

Tabetha and the Mungling led the way over dried lava flows, where rivers of stone had frozen hard as black ice. In places, the stone split wide and the glow of lava purred underneath.

While hopping over cracks and bubbling spouts of lava, the Mungling nattered on, as he was inclined to do when nervous. Tabetha felt nervous as well, and encouraged him.

"Tell me a story," she said. "Something to take my mind off this horrible place."

"A story about what?"

"I always like hearing about the Pump Dragons," she replied. "Tell me about them. Tell me about the dragons before they left Wrush."

"Ah, those were much happier days," the Mungling answered. "Even when the people of Wrush couldn't see them, the Pump Dragons presence was felt in the air. It was like sunlight— a radiance that fell everywhere, but was impossible to pinpoint or capture."

"Did the Pump Dragons always live in Wrush?" she asked.

"I don't know. Though I feel as if I should." The Mungling was quiet for moment, as if considering the question, then continued, "Where the dragons first came from, I can't say. But Wrush is where they lived for as long as anyone can remember, as Wrush is the only place their Noble Trees ever grew."

"The dragon's food?" asked Tabetha.

"That's right," said the Mungling. "The fruit of the Noble Tree was the only food rich enough to sustain the dragons. But there are legends of a dragon king, the first and greatest of them all. A mighty dragon named Azu Prekahn. It was Azu who led the

Pump Dragons through the Wink Holes of the universe, showering wisdom like rain upon each world they visited. So we know they traveled, or were wanderers of some sort. But the dragons always returned to Wrush for their Noble Trees."

"That's why Morlac cut them down, isn't it," Tabetha said. "He cut down the trees to shut the dragons out of Wrush, forcing them to dig Wink Holes to other worlds in search of food."

"Not just any other worlds, Tabetha," the Mungling replied. "Morlac needed the dragons to dig a Wink Hole to Earth, which is the universe's heart. That way he could bring his army of Gwybies through. A Wink Hole is the only tunnel that can pass directly to Earth, and Pump Dragons are the only creatures that can dig them."

Tabetha frowned. "This is a terrible story, Mungling. I was hoping for something to cheer me up. Now I'm more worried than ever."

"You're right, Tabetha. You deserve something far better. Ahh! Here's one you'll like!" And the Mungling told Tabetha a proper story this time, an old legend he called 'The Reckoning.' It was the story of Azu Prekkahn, most ancient of the Pump Dragons, and how he disappeared long ago on a significant quest. But the dragon king never returned. Where Azu had gone, and what he was looking for, no one knew. But the legend went on to say that one day, the great dragon would dig his last Wink Hole directly through the Hedge to Earth, and lead all the other dragons back to their Noble Trees.

"That's more like it," said Tabetha as the Mungling finished. "I like that kind of ending."

"Old Azu Prekahn," the Mungling whispered to himself, shaking his head with sweet longing. "What I wouldn't do to meet a king like that."

Toward the end of the story about Azu Prekahn, Tabetha was reminded of a dream she had— a dream of an old rounded hill that lay just back of her house. The hill was flushed blue with Forget-me-not flowers, and its memory, for some peculiar reason, always returned to Tabetha at the mention of Pump Dragons. Tabetha wondered at this now, the blue hill from her dream shining bright in her mind's eye.

"Mungling," she began, wanting to hear his thoughts on the matter.

"Yes, Tabetha?"

"I was wondering—"

But before Tabetha could continue, she was abruptly assaulted by a stench so powerful it knocked all thought from her head.

"Yuck!" she exclaimed, before she even realized she'd said it. The odor was so bad, it scorched the inside of her nose. "What is that terrible smell?"

The ground had become damp, and the mud belched and burned. Thick black fumes clung like smoke to the bogs.

"Never mind the smell," replied Answer, who was now walking beside them. "Beware of the quicksand." The wizard pointed to a pond of soupy looking clay. "The swamps of Tsepudra have swallowed goblins and worse. Leave the path now, and there's no telling what'll get you first."

So these were the Marshes of Krud, Tabetha thought. What a miserable dark hole of a place. As she peered through the reeking steam and mists, weariness fell down round her like an iron cloak. She was suddenly tired to the bone, and not just sleepy, but the sucking, draining exhaustion only her illness could create. Her legs ached, and even her arms were cramping. What she needed now was to sleep, to get down from this saddle and curl into bed for a week, but inside she knew there wasn't a moment to lose.

"Look at this, the Gwybies must be just ahead." Their claw-prints pressed and scraped all through the muck. Tabetha's captain frowned at the mess. There could be no doubt now: Thomas Morlac had chosen the same path to the pyramid— her path— and deep down inside, she felt a hard pit in her stomach, fearing what would happen when they met again. Thomas had at least a hundred monsters for every one of her friends, and the Bell-man's last words, as important as they seemed, could do nothing to protect her.

The Mungling stumbled.

Then began to slide.

Tabetha yelped from atop his saddle as they slipped slowly from the muddy bank to the water, the Mungling's feet sinking deeper and deeper in muck. "Help!" she cried from his back. "We're slipping!" But Isaac was there in an instant, tugging the Mungling free of the bog.

"You best be careful there, Mungling." Isaac steadied him, patting his chubby head with a soldier's roughness. "That's the empress on your back! No more precious cargo than her!"

Tabetha was too drained to thank him. She struggled to stay upright in the saddle. "Isaac," she called, and then swallowed, catching her breath. He would carry her if she asked. "Isaac," she said again, and then stopped suddenly, her ears perked to the night. *What's that sound?* She squinted through the fog.

Growling or something. Shrieks, she thought. *Not far away, and only one thing I know can made that sound.*

Isaac's eyes grew wide and hard. He drew his sword with a metallic whisper.

The shrieks grew louder, the mists lit with orange torches and Tabetha felt the overpowering urge to flee. Then Answer stepped calmly to her side.

"They heard me cry for help, didn't they?" Tabetha asked, already smelling the Gwybies approach.

Answer nodded, his eyes fixed on the mist. She felt his calm wash over her like warm milk. "It's not your fault, Tabetha. We knew it would come to this. We knew all along we would face them."

Energized with fear, Tabetha's breath came quick. The blood fluttered through her ears like moth wings. "They're getting closer," she panted, watching the torches grow brighter, feeling the Gwybies' shrieks prickling her skin. The mist swirled, and then something charged into the open. "They're here!" she gasped, gripping the leather reins tightly in her fists. "They're all around!"

The first of the Gwybies let out a blood-curdling howl, then sprinted toward her through the mud and the mist. Others took up the cry, first here, then there, then all around, rising like a circle of flames. Tabetha's skin went cold and she felt the Mungling tremble. Then all at once, from everywhere, Gwybies loped in from the fog. "They're coming!" she cried, slapping her thighs with raw panic. She could see their small eyes and the foul clouds of their breath. She turned to Answer.

His tattoos popped like flashbulbs.

His calm was thick as honey in the air.

"You needn't fear," he said, the hint of a smile in his voice. "You've no idea how we wizards greet a Gwybie."

"Never trust a creature whose teeth are bigger than its brain."

ireworks.

That's what it was like. Tabetha had never before seen wizards do battle. Sheets of flame tore down from the sky, spears of light splintered the earth. Everywhere she turned, Gwybies sputtered and roared and slapped out fires in their fur. The air hissed and screamed with blinding rockets.

"You must flee, My Lady!" Isaac shouted as he slashed at a Gwybie, then turned and blocked a spear thrust from another. "You must go! Mungling! Take the empress away!"

For every Gwybie that fell, five more replaced him. The swamp was alive with their shrieking.

"This way!" cried the Mungling, aiming to rush her through a gap in the battle. He started off at a gallop when a huge arm clamped down around Tabetha's shoulders. A Gwybie lifted her high in the air, his muscles hard as iron.

"No! Noooo!" Tabetha screamed as she beat against his enormous chest. She saw spittle leap from his fangs when he roared.

"Such a wiggly little morsel!" His voice screeched like fingernails down chalkboards. "Now let's see how she tastes!" He opened his mouth wide, his fangs foul and dripping, when a brick of light knocked him to his knees, senseless. The Gwybie swayed for a moment, dropped Tabetha in the mud and at last crumpled beside her like a house of cards.

Tabetha fought to get up, to get away. She grunted and pushed; she clawed at the earth but her arms were too weak, her legs useless as wood. She heard the sharp sound of a whistle and glanced up.

It was Answer. Her eyes found him, the silhouette of a boy upon higher ground, standing alone with arms outstretched. It was Answer who had saved her with his magic. She watched as a bolt of lightning leapt from his chest, crackling through a line of Gwybies. Others rushed forward as if there were no end to their numbers.

"Get on!" yelled the Mungling in her ear, and helped her into his saddle. Arrows of light zipped close overhead and blue fire rained down from above. Tabetha ducked instinctively, trying to strap herself in.

"I'm in!" she shouted, jolting backward as the Mungling took off. To her horror, he charged straight for a dense knot of

Gwybies. He hollered so loudly they startled like geese, but still they swiped at Tabetha's hair with their claws.

The Mungling burst through and then rounded a column of fire.

"I think I see Morlac!" Tabetha yelled above the din of battle. She turned her head, trying not to lose sight of him. She saw a Hinji, the giant black hyena he rode, jerk back from the chaos and flames. It yammered and spun, its teeth snapping at sparks. Atop its saddle was a rider in black.

"It is him! It is!"

"No time for that, Tabetha! Leave Morlac for Answer to deal with!"

"Where are you taking me?" she yelled.

"Somewhere safe if I can! But I'll settle for plain somewhere else!"

Tabetha could still hear the rumble of battle at her back, though it grew quieter as they ventured further into the swamps. The Mungling tromped on, uncharacteristically silent. Worried for her, probably. Just like Answer and Isaac, who were still fighting at this very moment to protect her and her purpose.

The mists were breaking up and the Marshes of Krud were slowly giving way to hard ground. Tabetha sensed she and the Mungling were moving gradually downhill.

"Do you think they'll be all right?" she asked. A hard knot in her belly told her something was very wrong.

The Mungling said nothing for a time. His footsteps sounded loud in the dark. "There were many Gwybies back there, Tabetha. More than I've ever seen. But if anyone could survive, it's those two."

"But do you think they will?" she persisted.

"I don't know, Tabetha. I only know they would both gladly do it all again to keep you safe."

She knew this was true. Her heart filled till it ached.

"Even so," she said after some thought. "I want to wait for them at the bottom of this hill. At least for a little while."

"They'll want you to keep on," the Mungling argued. "That's what they're fighting for. They'll want you to find the first pyramid, with or without them."

This too Tabetha knew was true. If only she didn't feel like she'd deserted them. She trudged along with the Mungling, weighted with guilt and exhaustion, trying to swallow back the sour taste on her tongue.

For no reason at all, she thought of her pen. Her magic pen. An image of its finely polished wood sprang to mind, but it was quickly replaced by Thomas's last warning: *the ink is running out.* The pen's magic was near its end. How many more times would the pen carry her back to Wrush? What would she do when the ink ran out?

She didn't know, and worry piled upon worry in her head.

"Do you smell that?" the Mungling suddenly asked, lifting his nose to the air. "Bells and pumpkins, what a stink! What is that?"

Tabetha had no idea. "It's nothing like before," she said,

pinching her nose. "Not Gwybies. Not swamps. This smell is more like . . . garbage."

The smell grew stronger as they reached the bottom of the hill, and all at once Tabetha realized where they were.

"The Pits of Prantis," she said aloud, checking her whereabouts against the map. "It's where the pyramid is supposed to be."

There were no trees or brush of any kind. The ground was baked and cracked and strewn with rocks, both large and small. As they walked on, great depressions emerged, ugly craters and vents of red steam.

"Reminds me of pictures I've seen of the moon," she told the Mungling, who asked if the moon stunk like a city dump.

"Not that I recall reading," she said. "But look there. No, right in front of us. What is that?"

She pointed. Not far ahead, a collection of trash towered so high as to be mistaken for a pointy hill in the dark. Only when distant volcanoes blew their top, and the sky glowed red did the great heap reveal itself as pure trash.

"Well that explains the smell," the Mungling observed. "Looks like a pile of trash."

"More like a mountain of trash, if you ask me. Sort of strange, don't you think? To find such a thing here, in the middle of nowhere?"

"Not nowhere, Tabetha. *Tsepudra.*"

How could she forget? Tsepudra. The ugliest of all worlds if Answer was right, and now here Tabetha was in the worst of it.

As they drew closer, Tabetha's eyes picked out oilcans and fish bones, curdled buckets of sludge. There were reptilian skins, and old bean tins, and black sharks' fins and tails. Every possible kind of scrap and litter, black and putrid, rotted there inside the heap, melting into hairy slime like November pumpkins on the porch. Tabetha was in a state of horrified marvel.

"I've never seen such a disgusting heap!"

Then, to her greater surprise, what she thought was a nearby boulder stood up on four legs, clacked its huge teeth and growled.

"Oh dear," said the Mungling, backing slowly away. "Better hold on there, Tabetha."

"What is it?" She shuddered, clutching the reins to her chest. "What is that thing?"

She saw a mouth. She saw teeth. She saw two pair of legs. And that was all, nothing more. Whatever this beast was, it was built for eating and little else.

As the creature lurched forward, Tabetha saw it lick its thick lips. She saw no eyes, but from the way the thing grinned she knew it could sense her.

"It's a Burbleglock," said the Mungling, swallowing so loud she could hear it. "The hungriest creature in all the universe."

ℒ

A word to the wise.

Should you ever find yourself needing to charm a cobra, do not waste time learning the flute. Snakes have no ears and are therefore deaf. Instead, take any object at the ready— a pork chop, a calculator, a squeaky toy from your dog— and rock it in a side-to-side motion before the serpent, for it is in fact only the movement of the charmer's flute, and not the sound, that holds a cobra's attention.

But be warned: The cobra may enjoy this greatly and wish to express its affection. You must, however, avoid its kiss at all costs. I will teach you.

First, place your own arm flat on a table. That's right. Now, keeping your elbow there, bend your arm so that your hand rises up as a hooded cobra would.

Perfect.

Now let it drop.

You have just demonstrated a cobra's strike, and so long as your elbow remains in contact with the table, you will notice how your hand always falls forward and down, forward and down, and always at a predictable distance. It is exactly the same for a cobra. Though he may strike more to the left or more to the right, depending on where you place your pork chop/calculator/rubber kitten, he will never strike at a distance greater than his standing height. It is your job to remain beyond this border.

Of course there is one other option, which is simply to feed the cobra a mouse, for a snake with its mouth full poses no danger. Coincidentally, Tabetha knew something of snakes, and as you shall soon see, charming a Burbleglock would not be so very different.

From what she could tell, a Burbleglock was nothing but a huge and hideous mouth with four legs and sharp teeth, each as long and drippy as spring icicles. It was, no matter how generously she described it, not a very handsome animal.

"The Burbleglock thinks we've come to steal his food," whispered the Mungling, still creeping slowly backward.

"What food?" asked Tabetha. "We haven't come to take anything."

"The trash heap," hissed the Mungling. "It's where Burbleglocks feed. There aren't any more Burbleglocks in Wrush because they've eaten themselves to extinction. When a Burbleglock runs out of food, he'll eat anything. Even himself!"

The creature stood tall as a tractor and walked with a swinging motion from side-to-side, his legs bent at the knees like a lizard's. He grinned again, smacking his lips with delight.

"Come here little foodlings! Come to my mouth!"

And with these words it seemed suddenly possible that Burbleglocks, despite their spectacular appetites, might not be too bright in the head.

"Ohhh! You are to be so juicy and crunchable! Is it true?" The Burbleglock shuddered with anticipation, slobbering all over himself.

"No," said Tabetha. "We're just visiting, and it's not polite to eat your visitors."

This stopped him dead. He stood frozen with indecision.

"You've thrown him for a loop, Tabetha!" she heard the Mungling whisper. "He's got no idea what to do now!"

But then the Burbleglock lumbered forward, still drooling and grinning. "Would you like to pat my tummy?" he asked.

There was something so pathetic, so outrageously dumb about this creature that Tabetha was almost tempted to try.

"Don't do it!" hissed the Mungling. Then added, "Never trust a creature whose teeth are bigger than its brain. What they don't understand, they eat!"

"All right," announced Tabetha, more cautiously this time. "You seem to have quite an appetite, I see."

The Burbleglock bounced like a child in his excitement. "Oh yes, an appetite! To eat!"

Tabetha paused. "In that case, I challenge you to an eating contest. Let's see who can eat the biggest . . ." She looked around, searching the ground.

" . . . Rock," she said aloud. "Let's see who can eat the biggest rock."

The Burbleglock was all too happy to accept.

"I'll start," said Tabetha, and had the Mungling hand her a pebble. She opened her mouth and dropped it in. She swallowed. "There. See if you can top that."

The Burbleglock bent down and bit hold of a rock about the size of Tabetha's head. He crunched away, grinning, small clouds of powdered stone squirting from his jaws.

"Wow, that was pretty big," said Tabetha. "But see if you can beat this."

She had the Mungling give her another pebble, this one slightly larger than the first. She saved up some spit in her mouth, and then washed down the pebble with a gulp, telling herself that swallowing small rocks was better than being swallowed. Besides, at eight years of age Tabetha could claim very

few skills, so it felt good to see one of them at least (her exper-
tise with pills) had finally proven useful in a pinch.

"My turn! My turn!" cheered the Burbleglock, and Tabetha
watched him throw back another stone, this one noticeably
larger.

"Boy, I guess you Burbleglocks are pretty handy with those
teeth. But I'll bet you couldn't eat that one." She pointed to a
fair-sized boulder.

Without hesitation, the Burbleglock shambled to it and then
swallowed it down with glee. Tabetha noticed his shape was
changing. He was getting sort of bulgy, hanging low in the center the way lions do after a heavy feeding.

"That was incredible!" she declared. "I had no idea you Burbleglocks were so talented."

The Burbleglock licked his lips.

Tabetha smiled faintly. "Now, if you can eat *that* rock right
there . . . well, I'll be about as impressed as any person could be."

Tabetha pointed to the biggest, heaviest, most angular boulder in all the Pits of Prantis. It was ridiculously huge, nearly
the same size as the creature, and as he approached the rock
Tabetha felt a lopsided grin take hold of her mouth.

A curious shiver ran down her spine.

Now, Tabetha was quite a fan of nature documentaries. She
subscribed to a channel that showed nothing else. She watched
them for hours, alone in her bed. She'd seen sea turtles dig nests
and an octopus squirt ink, and even learned all about a carnivo-
rous green plant from Venus.

One show, however, was her favorite. Each time she saw it

she laughed herself silly. It was about a certain kind of snake that ate only eggs. The African Egg Eater he was called. Sort of skinny and long, with a head no bigger than a walnut. This snake would hunt around all day, slipping through brush and popping into holes until he came across his most favorite food in the world:

Eggs.

Heron's eggs, ostrich eggs, he would eat them all, whatever he could find. And whenever the African Egg Eater would find an egg, he'd get so excited he'd start flicking his tongue like a gypsy yodeler and nudging the egg about in its nest. But that wasn't even the best part. Watching this snake trying to swallow its prize sent Tabetha into something close to hysterics. You can imagine his challenge if you imagine yourself with your hands tied behind your back, a giant egg in your mouth, trying to swallow it all at once without chewing.

The African Egg Eater had figured out a pretty handy trick. It went something like this. The snake would open his jaws as wide as a hippo's yawn, then start scraping his teeth down the side of the egg trying to get a grip, which, as Tabetha noted in her diary, "*...is pretty hard when you can't just stuff it in like popcorn because evolution took all your knuckles away.*" So the snake would unhinge his jaws, allowing him to stretch his whole head around the egg, which was absolutely huge in comparison, and made the African Egg Eater look like a balloon about to burst.

In all her life, Tabetha had never dreamed she'd actually see such an amazing sight as the exotic, untamed African Egg Eater squeezing tremendous objects through its head, and yet here she was, in the fiery wastes of Tsepudra, watching a Burbleglock attempt this very feat.

She was enthralled.

The Burbleglock began by sidling up to the boulder, sniffing it once or twice like a fancy dish. Then he began trying to work his jaws around the boulder, just like the African Egg Eater and its egg. And like the egg, this boulder was simply too big, an impossible morsel that looked as if it would never fit. Yet he tried.

The Burbleglock groaned and he strained, his mouth stretching so wide it was sure to tear. Tabetha was white-knuckled with anticipation. Her own lips hung ajar, slightly curled in disgust, her eyes glued to the scene before her. This was better than documentaries. This was . . . this was . . .

"Amazing," she whispered aloud when the Burbleglock finished. She felt like a whole new person for having seen it.

The Burbleglock, once shaped like a mouth with four legs, was now shaped like a boulder. He couldn't move. He couldn't stand. The boulder inside his gut was so huge he couldn't even close his mouth properly, yet those lips could still grin in triumph.

"You're incredible," said Tabetha, her voice filled with wonder. "Absolutely incredible. I really don't know what to say. You win. You beat me by a mile."

Unable to speak, the Burbleglock continued to grin.

"Well," said Tabetha. "I think I'll remember you for the rest of my life. If all Burbleglocks are as entertaining as you, I think it's a shame there are no more left in Wrush. But I have to go now.

I'd ask you which way to the pyramid, but your mouth is quite full and I doubt you would be so rude as to answer. I guess I'll just have to look for myself."

With that, Tabetha and the Burbleglock— the hungriest, most atrocious creature in all the known universe— shared a parting smile, and then she was gone, the Burbleglock waving at her back.

Somewhere nearby was a pyramid just waiting to be found.

⌇

But they didn't make it very far, Tabetha and the Mungling. They found themselves oddly drawn to the enormous trash heap, now staring up at it with a mixture of revulsion and awe. It was huge and awful. Magnificent in the most terrible way.

Tabetha puffed the hair from her eyes and turned aside. They were already in the Pits of Prantis. So where could this pyramid possibly be?

During the crimson flash of a volcano, the Mungling glanced back over his shoulder at the Burbleglock, still pinned to the ground by his prize. "You know, you have quite a way with dangerous creatures, Tabetha." Perhaps he was remembering her encounter with the Thwork. Or maybe the Grimpkins. Or the salamander.

Which reminded her: When was she going to figure out this whole salamander key thing? Here she was in Tsepudra, with the first pyramid somewhere nearby, and she still hadn't solved this little creature's mystery. How could it be both a salamander and a key? She dipped a hand into her pocket and stroked his soft back.

And then there were the Bellman's mysterious parting words. If only he'd said more. If only he'd explained what he meant.

Only beauty knows beauty.

She'd thought it through a hundred times and still it made no sense. It seemed her questions might never get answered. Tabetha sighed, rubbed a cramp in her thigh. As she stared up at the trash heap, thinking few things could be less beautiful, she began to wonder if she was going about it all wrong. Maybe beauty wasn't a thing at all.

Maybe it was a time. Or even a place. Yeah, a place! But then if it were a place, she decided, certainly everyone would want to live there, and so far as Tabetha knew people lived just about anywhere.

No, beauty couldn't be a place.

Tabetha closed her eyes, tipped her face to the sky.

Unless . . .

She thought of a rose. She pictured it clearly in her mind. Where exactly was the loveliness in it? Was it in the petals? The stem? Could scientists find it with a microscope and cut it away?

Or— and this thought came out of nowhere— *or*, was the beauty of a rose simply that place in her heart, the place that flares like a match head when she sees it?

Tabetha was on to something. She could feel her pulse quicken. Her thoughts became vivid and spacious. Perhaps beauty was nothing she could touch or see. Perhaps it was a part of herself.

Maybe, she thought with a knowing smile, *it's that place inside me that sees things as they really are.*

-*Only beauty knows beauty*-

She opened her eyes.

The first pyramid stood towering before her.

Tabetha's heart plunged into blackness.

*Y*ou must wonder, dear reader, what it is like to have such a treasure revealed in this way; to be gazing upon a mountain of rubbish, a creature's foul hoard, and in a single moment find it transformed into an enchanted pyramid.

So I will tell you. But since there are no words in our language to express it, you must study the spaces between them, here on this page. That's right, the spaces between the letters themselves. For in the strange white shapes they form is hidden a second alphabet wherein I have described Tabetha's experience in full.

I understand there will be those among you too lazy to try, so I will explain this much: Looking upon the pyramid before her, Tabetha understood that it had always been there, exactly as she saw it now. But like my secret alphabet, it had lain hidden till she looked in just the right way.

Tabetha drew a long breath, noting a new freshness to the air. She exhaled and felt prickles of excitement.

It seemed the Bellman could not have given her better advice after all. It was only when she found beauty within that she could find it without, and it was this secret alone that disguised the pyramid from others.

"I see it too!" the Mungling suddenly declared.

Tabetha patted his neck. "I'm sure you do." Perhaps everyone could see it now that the spell had been broken. This delighted her. Then with a sinking feeling, Tabetha realized everyone meant *everyone*— even Thomas Morlac and his Gwybies would see it now.

"Come on," she said. "We'd better hurry."

Against the night sky, the pyramid stood illuminated by some unknown source. A golden gate was carved into the front. Sparkling beams spilled out, wherein gold dust floated like tiny stars. On a whim, the Mungling galloped forward until they entered its soft light. The sparkles clung to their skin and melted there. Then they were passing beneath the arch of the gate.

Tabetha shielded her eyes from the glow as they entered. She squinted and blinked, as if lost in a blizzard, waiting for her eyes to adjust. When at last she could see, she found that they were in a room. To her surprise, Tabetha knew this place. She had been here before.

Every inch of the room's walls was covered with clocks. The orchestra of their ticking was the only sound. There were brass clocks and gold clocks and clocks carved from dark wood. Clocks even hung from the ceiling, their long rhythmic clangors sweeping side-to-side so that the entire room appeared in a state of movement.

"It's not exactly what I expected," she heard the Mungling say. "What kind of place is this?"

Through a small, high window, a single pale ray cast dusty light over a worktable covered with countless tiny gears, sprockets, small gleaming tools, and magnifying glasses: Clock parts. Tabetha and the Mungling were in the same repair shop she had once visited with her father when he'd gone to pick up his watch. The shop owner had misplaced the watch among the countless timepieces, and she had sat in her father's lap for close to an hour, waiting while the little owner bustled about in search of it. Tabetha wondered if she was actually in the shop now, or if the pyramid's inner chamber was a room pieced together from her past, made of memories entirely her own.

"It's so strange," she said. "I was here when I was five. Nothing especially fun or exciting happened, but I've always remembered this place for some reason."

Tabetha glanced about. Behind her was the door that led back to Tsepudra, although it now appeared to open onto a street. Through its glass she could see people passing on the pavement beyond. Around her, the room ticked and tocked. It smelled of clock oil and dust. And then, all at once, every clock came to a perfect halt. In the silence that followed, an enormous grandfather clock at the end of the room began to chime.

Bong.

Bong.

Bong.

The tall body of the clock was carved into the shape of a dragon. Slowly, the Mungling crept toward it, Tabetha clutching the reins on his back.

Bong.

Bong.

Bong.

When the Mungling reached the grandfather clock, the chiming ceased.

"Wow," Tabetha whispered. She felt the hairs rise on the back of her neck. At last, after countless miles and untold dangers, after restless nights and days full of worry, Tabetha Bright and the Mungling were finally inside the first of the Three Guardians, the Pyramid of Tsepudra, facing the task they had so long awaited.

She reached deep into her pocket. Felt the salamander grow warm.

Only one thing remained to be done.

$\mathcal{E}_{\mathcal{C}}$

In almost the same way that you, dear reader, can flip through these pages and know Part One of this book is fast approaching the end, Tabetha was overcome with a jittery anticipation. What's more, she sensed something very special was about to take place, right there in the repair shop, hidden within the pyramid's inner chamber. An event that had everything to do with the magical creature in her pocket.

She stroked the salamander, yet her eyes were drawn to the

grandfather clock, which stood taller than herself, the ancient timepiece fashioned into a dragon. Even Tabetha could tell the workmanship was beyond any artist on Earth. In polished black wood, the dragon reared up like a stallion in battle, its wings neatly tucked, its gleaming head held high like a king of kings.

"A Pump Dragon," the Mungling said after recovering his voice. "And not just any of them. That's a carving of Old Azu Prekahn, first and greatest of them all."

A picture of the blue hill came to Tabetha's mind. She was lying atop it. She felt the salamander in her pocket grow warmer.

She removed the salamander and held him up in her palm. He immediately began walking toward the tips of her fingers. She placed her other hand in front to catch him, but the salamander simply kept walking.

"It's like he's trying to get somewhere," the Mungling observed. "He's not the least bit afraid of falling."

Tabetha continued to rotate her hands, offering the flat surface of each palm when the salamander reached the edge. "Pretty determined, isn't he. It's like he knows where he's going." Tabetha looked up, her eyes meeting the dragon's. A soft feeling passed through her heart. "It's like he's trying to get to the clock. To Azu Prekahn."

Tabetha and the Mungling shared a knowing look. Neither spoke. As if by instruction, her eyes drifted to the Pump Dragon's chest, where she noticed the seams of a door hiding the clock's inner workings. It had been cunningly crafted, almost invisible at first glance, but cut into the door was the unmistakable outline of a . . .

"Is that . . ." Her eyes narrowed. "Is that a *keyhole*?"

It was shaped like one at least, even if it was larger than most. Tabetha thought she could probably squeeze her whole hand into that slot.

"It sure looks like a keyhole," replied the Mungling. "Are you thinking what I'm thinking?"

Slowly, carefully, Tabetha lifted the salamander to the height of the keyhole. His red skin glowed bright in response.

Tabetha licked her lips, her excitement swelling. She breathed hard through her mouth. The salamander skittered forward as if he'd rehearsed for this moment. He peeked into the keyhole, turned back once in farewell, and then disappeared into the door of the clock.

So that's how a salamander can be both a salamander and a key.

All at once, the dragon's chest flared red, as if a fire burned within. The salamander had gone ablaze, just as he had in the desert. Rays of light streamed through the keyhole. Then the Mungling jolted and jumped back in surprise, for the Pump Dragon's mouth began to open.

"He is the key!" Tabetha cried. "The salamander is the key, and he's unlocking the pyramid's magic!"

But then the salamander's fire went out, the repair shop suddenly dimmed, and everything went terribly wrong.

Directly behind her, Tabetha heard the chiming of the door's bells, then the eerie padding of a hyena's paws across wood. The Mungling wheeled toward the entrance, gasping in dismay. Tabetha's stomach twisted tight.

An enormous black Hinji faced them in the gloom, Thomas

Morlac sitting astride its saddle. His cape was of midnight, his helmet black pitch. She heard him chuckle softly to himself before lifting his visor.

"I warned you, Tabetha." His eyes were hard and cold. "I told you to stay out of my way. I'm taking this pyramid, whether you like or not."

Tabetha pursed her lips and scowled. "You're no sorcerer, just a mean little boy. As soon as Answer and Isaac get here, they'll show you."

"Your wizard?" sneered Morlac. "And your captain? They're already here. You want to see them?"

Morlac motioned with his arm, and Tabetha instinctively cringed as a dozen of his Gwybies entered through the door, not one person on the street taking notice. Instantly, the room filled with the Gwybies' stink.

"Gwybies," he said calmly. "Show Tabetha her friends."

With a great clatter, a single hairy arm swept the contents of the worktable to the floor. Answer and Isaac were dumped roughly atop it, tied together, back to back.

"No!" Tabetha cried. It couldn't be! To her horror, their hands were bound, their mouths stuffed with cloth. It didn't seem possible that her friends could be captured.

Yet here they were on the table, prisoners, helpless as birds in a cage, and Tabetha's heart plunged into blackness.

$\mathcal{C}\iota$

So here they were again, just like in the hospital— *Face-to-face with my enemy,* Tabetha thought with a dread chill. Unable to turn from Morlac's icy glare, she couldn't help but recall their last showdown in their bedroom, the one she had failed when she spilled her medicine.

"Here's your High Wizard of Wrush, Tabetha. Your brave captain, too." Morlac turned to her friends, peering down at them with disgust from high in his saddle. "Look at them, Tabetha. They're wimps. They're weaklings." He faced her. "Even so, I know they're all you had. And now they're mine."

Tabetha glanced at Isaac on his knees, then Answer beside him. She expected to see fear, its tight lines in their faces. Instead she found a fierce gleam in their eyes.

"Tabetha," Morlac said, padding forward on his Hinji. The enormous hyena's eyes burned into her. "Tabetha, give me the magic of this pyramid. Whatever you've found here, it's mine now." He halted, towering above her in his saddle. "Give it to me, or this will be the last you'll ever see of your friends."

"I don't have anything," Tabetha protested. "I've taken nothing from the pyramid."

Morlac paused, waiting to see if she'd say more. When she didn't, he twisted slowly back to his monsters.

"Gwybies! Take the prisoners outside. Eat the big one if you like, but save the wizard for me. I have something special in store for him."

"Wait!" Tabetha yelled in a panic. "Wait! There's . . . there's more."

Morlac halted the Gwybies with a hand, and then shifted in his saddle to face Tabetha, a wry grin on his face. "Go on," he taunted, and Tabetha swallowed hard against the lump in her throat.

"I know more," she said in a strangled whisper.

He chuckled. "Good. Let's hear it. Tell me where the pyramid's magic is hidden."

Hesitantly, Tabetha turned her head to the grandfather clock against the wall. The salamander was no longer ablaze. It had doused itself the moment Morlac came into the room. She pointed to the keyhole carved into the clock's body and Morlac gasped with unconcealed joy.

"There?" he said, pointing as well, as if unable to believe his good luck. "There, inside that keyhole? That's where the magic is hidden?"

It wasn't a lie when Tabetha nodded. He had asked for hidden magic, and that's what he'd get. She had simply left out a small part.

Morlac urged his mount forward, forcing Tabetha and the Mungling aside. He paused only a moment before thrusting his arm to the elbow inside the dragon's chest. His whole face tightened with concentration as he groped about inside the clock, then it brightened, eyes wide, as his hand closed around something small.

And soft.

"Aha!" he hissed in triumph, then withdrew his fist from the keyhole. He opened it to find a little red creature, eyes friendly and large, staring back at him. A feeling of gentle surprise registered on the sorcerer's face. For an instant, he appeared thoughtful, quieted, wondrously tender— even peaceful. And then the salamander burst into a ball of howling flame.

Whuuuump!

The flames whined in Morlac's hand and he yelped, tossing the salamander on reflex. He swatted the air, as though at invisible flies, trying desperately to put out the pain.

"It's a trick!" he hollered, his face red with rage. "She tricked us! Don't let her escape!"

The Gwybies flashed their long fangs and slashed at the air with their claws. Several of them advanced on Tabetha.

But even before Tabetha could cry out, something unexpected took place. The salamander, it seemed, had grown angry. No longer a small ball of fire, it swelled into a crackling orb of light. It hissed and it sizzled, it screamed and spat suns. Everyone present gaped in astonishment.

Then, without warning, the orb exploded with a CRACK! and the thunder of it slapped Gwybies against the wall. It singed the hair on their tongues and shook the teeth clean from their heads. The bells within every clock rang at once while streamers of electric confetti whizzed in all directions, terrifying the monsters to no end. They rushed wailing through the door with Morlac's Hinji quick on their heels, swarms of angry light chasing them like wasps.

When the room cleared of smoke and only the smell of burnt hair lingered in the silence, the Mungling cranked his head around to Tabetha. He wore a look of surprise. "You're not hurt?"

She shook her head. "Not at all. The salamander never meant to hurt *us*."

Tabetha and the Mungling turned together toward the sound of muffled shouts.

"Answer! Isaac!" The Mungling rushed Tabetha to their friends and unbound their ties. Answer rubbed the dents in his wrists as he caught his breath.

"Where's the salamander?" was the first thing he asked.

Each of them glanced around. There was no sign of it anywhere. Then Tabetha reached back into her pocket.

"Look," she said, holding out her hand. Two soft little balls of jelly clung to the life-line in her palm. "Salamander eggs. He gave his own life to protect us, and left only these behind."

Answer peered closer, even nudged a tiny sticky egg with his finger. "Appears so," he said. "I guess *he* was a *she*, and very brave at that. We'll have to get these eggs into water before they spoil." After a moment's thought, he added, "I'm grateful for the salamander's help. She saved us all. But it is a shame we never found out why Wrushic Salamanders are called keys. Rare as they are, I would like to have known."

That's when Tabetha remembered.

"But we did!" she cheered. "We did find out. The salamander unlocked the Pump Dragon's mouth!"

She explained quickly before Isaac, being tallest, went to the clock. With one arm, he reached up into the dragon's mouth and pulled something white and polished from the open jaws.

"What do think this is?" he asked as he turned it over in his hand, bringing it near for all to see.

Answer pinched the small object between his fingers and held it above his head, turning the item in wonder. "Legends alive," he whispered to himself. For he understood what no one else did: He, Tabetha, Isaac, and the Mungling, were the first people in over ten thousand years to gaze upon the cold gleam of a Puzzle Bead.

At first no one spoke, as the idea seemed too silly . . .

Puzzle Bead, you ask? *What could that be?*
Only the most magical item in the universe.

Tabetha held it carefully in her hand. It was a beautiful item, etched with designs, white as ivory and cut at one end in the jigsaw manner of puzzles.

"That jagged end there fits into another just like it," Answer explained. "There are three Puzzle Beads in all. One from each pyramid. Plug them all together and they form a tooth. A Pump Dragon's tooth. None other than the great fang stolen long ago from Old Azu Prekahn, and used in the magic that keeps him and his brothers this side of the Hedge."

"You mean—" A sudden cough interrupted Tabetha before she could finish. She cleared her throat, regaining her breath with some effort. "You mean," she continued, "that a single tooth from the king of the Pump Dragons was cut into three pieces, then hidden in each of the Three Pyramids?"

Answer nodded. "It's that very magic that forms the Hedge."

"And if Morlac ever gets all three pieces of the tooth?"

"He can fit them together," Answer said, "and destroy the magical wall that protects Earth from the rest of the universe."

Tabetha's decision came easy. "Then we have to hide it," she said, stifling another cough. "We need to get this Puzzle Bead back to Etherios where we can bury it in the deepest dungeon."

"That's the first place Morlac will look," replied Answer. "It's the way we sorcerers think."

"Then cast it into the Conundric River," Isaac proposed. "Or the belly of one of Tsepudra's volcanoes."

Answer shook his head. "Neither of those would stop a sorcerer either."

"Can we break it?" asked Tabetha.

"Impossible."

"What then?"

The Mungling scratched at his shoulder where the saddle often chafed. "How about if Tabetha wears it around her neck?" he suggested.

At first no one spoke, as the idea seemed too silly. There was nothing safe about keeping the Puzzle Bead on hand, toting it about like jewelry. But as the friends talked further, it began to make more and more sense. If Tabetha wore a Puzzle Bead around her neck, like some little girl's charm, no one would ever suspect its real value. Not even Morlac, as he still didn't know exactly what the thing he searched for looked like.

So it was decided. Isaac snapped a leather cord from his own neck and tied the Puzzle Bead in place. He slipped it gently over Tabetha's head. "There. Now you've got the crown of an empress, and the most valuable necklace in the universe. Quite the accessories, I think."

For just a kid, Tabetha thought with an inner smile, wondering if anyone her age even dreamed of such ornaments.

Answer said, "So long as it stays hidden around your neck, and free from Morlac's grasp, we'll have little to worry about, Tabetha. Yet I think it's wise to collect the next two Puzzle Beads as well. There's no point in letting Morlac have them."

"I'm for it," said Isaac with a soldier's gusto.

"Me too!" chirped the Mungling. "What are we waiting for?"

They all looked to Tabetha. She glanced at her watch. She still had hours before she needed to be back for her medicine, which was perhaps plenty of time to track down the second pyramid. But she knew she couldn't.

"I'm so sorry," she apologized. "I want to. So badly I do, but..."

"It's okay, Tabetha," Answer put his arm around her, once again the older brother she loved. "Though you haven't complained once," he said, "we know you're not well. We can see it in you. You can barely sit up in your saddle. If it were up to me, I would have had you stop to rest long ago, but as you said, you made a promise to yourself. Which you've kept, I'll have you know, so there's no reason to feel bad about returning to Earth now."

Answer was right, she knew. Tabetha was *not* well, and truth be told she was more than a little frightened for her health. She couldn't remember ever having felt this weak, even when the illness was at its worst.

"I'll return to my own world and rest then," she said. "But the moment I'm stronger, I promise, I'm coming straight back."

Answer smiled brightly, if not a little sadly. "No need to promise, Tabetha. We know you'll come back."

"What about the salamander's eggs?" asked Isaac. "They're sure to grow into two more salamanders. The very keys we'll need to unlock the Puzzle Beads in the remaining pyramids."

"You're right," said Tabetha, dipping into her pocket. "What should I do with them?"

"Take them with you," said Answer. "Put them in water and in time they'll hatch. I'll look forward to seeing what the young ones look like when you come back."

"So you're leaving now?" asked the Mungling.

Tabetha nodded sadly. "I think I need to. Something's not right inside. For a while there I was feeling better, but now, even with the medicine the doctors are saying . . .they think . . ." She paused. She opened her mouth to say more, but couldn't finish.

"No need to talk about that now, Tabetha." The Mungling patted her kindly. "Just hurry back soon as you can, because we'll miss you here. We always do."

He reached into his saddlebag and retrieved a sheet of paper. He gave it to Tabetha along with a clipboard he now carried for this very purpose. "Here you go," he said. "Write your way home. And don't worry about us. Answer already said he's figured out a way to get us back through the World Bell."

"You did?" she asked. "I wondered about that."

Answer nodded. "A good wizard only needs to see magic work once before he can repeat the same spell. There was nothing particularly difficult about what the Bellman did."

"Well, I guess this is it then," said Tabetha, taking up her magic pen in one hand. She set the tip against paper. She wrote her first line and . . .

Nothing happened.

Tabetha stared at the blank paper in disbelief, her heart pounding somewhere near her throat. The Mungling's face became a picture of worry. "Probably just the weather," he offered, his voice trembling and overly cheerful. "Sometimes that happens with pens, you know, when the weather's too wet or too dry."

But Tabetha knew different. She already knew the pen's ink was running out, and what's more, she knew what would happen if she couldn't get back.

No medicine.

She glanced at Isaac, then Answer. Neither looked hopeful. At last the boy-wizard spoke, breaking the worrisome silence. "Give it a shake, Tabetha. Shake the pen up and down some."

She had already thought of that, but was almost too afraid to try. If shaking it didn't work, then nothing else would. Her doom would become sealed. She stared at the pen in her hand, trying to calm her racing thoughts. At last she took a deep breath and shook it, two stiff jerks up and down.

"Keep going. A little more," said Answer. "Just shake it up and down really hard."

Tabetha shook the pen as if her life depended on it, which in fact it did. She put the pen to the paper and began scribbling, almost frantically, with nothing coming out, and then, as glorious as first water pumped from a desert well, ink gushed from the tip in a glowing streak.

Everyone sighed with relief. The Mungling laughed nervously. Tabetha's hands wouldn't stop trembling. She looked up, meeting each of her friend's eyes, wondering if everyone understood what this meant.

Her passages to Wrush were limited, and no one knew exactly how many were left.

"It seems to be going fine now," she said, her voice straining through a quiver. And then to reassure herself, added, "Now that I know the trick, I should be able to get the pen working when I need to."

She took another breath and set to work writing. And though the pen's magic worked, and carried her gently back home, and though the welcome of white sheets was soft as ever, Tabetha Bright did not return home in peace.

Upon arriving, she immediately placed the salamander eggs in what remained of a cup of water, and then slipped the cup into the darkness of her bedside drawer. Beside them she placed her jar of frowns, still uncertain what use they could be. She then tucked the Puzzle Bead beneath the collar of her pajama blouse and lastly, she returned her magic pen to its box which she hid beneath the mattress. Hearing familiar movement on the far side of the room, she yanked back the curtains from her bed.

It was no small thing, Tabetha concluded with a sigh, this business of sharing one's room with sworn enemies.

Part Two

Author's Note

*O*once told you, what now seems long ago, how a star burns brightest just before it dies out. In a mighty explosion of light it grows to many times its own size, swallowing darkness and even the planets about it. And then in the blink of an eye, between the beats of a heart, it is gone. The star is quenched like a candle's wick in the breeze.

Make no mistake. Tabetha is that star. The great event I promised is now at hand. The day she changed the world is at last recorded in this book, and even the stones shall be moved when all is told.

Do not fear this end.

If you fear, I cannot teach you.

My name is The Karakul.

"Mom, when am I going home?"

As you well know by now, I am an old man, as kindly and tolerant as they come. You know also I have many secrets, and some of them I have gladly shared. This next one, however, does not pass easily from my pen, if only because it is so dear. Yet I shall put it here:

No one can have less than they truly need.

But wait! Consider this deeply before you disagree. For every person on Earth there are approximately one million ants, and every one of them knows these words to be true. It is a fact known to all ravens, and to every fish in the sea.

And as you will soon observe, even when deprived of all but her heart, Tabetha will have everything she ever required to be free.

So come with me now. Let us finish this journey. Let us join

Tabetha, lying upon her bed for the very last time, flushed red in the cheeks, in the dreary lamplight of her old hospital room.

$\mathcal{C}$

"Now hold real still for me, okay?" said the nurse.

Tabetha winced. She did her best not to cry out. She clenched her teeth, sucking in a hiss as the nurse slipped the needle into her arm. There was a sharp pinch, a dull ache, and then it was over. Tabetha opened her eyes as the nurse stretched a short ribbon of tape across her forearm to hold the IV in place.

"There you go, dear. All done," the nurse said in a soothing voice, brushing the hair from Tabetha's eyes. She lifted her arm, inspecting the tiny, clear tube of the IV. It curled up and away from her skin, attaching to a bag of liquid medicine hanging from a pole above her bed. It didn't really hurt, it was just . . . *weird*, to look up and see medicine trickling down through a tube into her body.

Tabetha should be used to it, she supposed: the daily needle pokes, the thermometers, the pressure cuffs closing like heavy fingers about her arm. So many strange beeps and devices she'd grown familiar with here in the hospital, but these IV's— these tangles of spiraling tubes were somehow different, and somehow more threatening when she stopped to think about them.

Tabetha's arm flopped to the sheets. She was getting sicker. She didn't need plastic tubes to tell her so. Over the past two weeks, since her return from Wrush and the finding of the first pyramid, Tabetha had felt worse in her body than she could ever remember. Her muscles had grown so weak that even breathing made her tired, and sometimes she skipped meals just to sleep. Why wasn't her medicine helping?

In these moments of despair it had become a new habit of hers to touch the Puzzle Bead that hung about her neck. It reassured her. It was good to know at least this much was safe. To know this much of the Hedge was beyond Thomas's grasp. Even if he did find the others, he would need to fit all three beads together, and Tabetha meant to see that it never happened.

Presently, she glanced across the room, her eyes taking in the rumpled sheets of his bed. His aluminum crutches crossed like a pair of long scissors and leaned against the wall by his dresser. But Thomas Morlac was nowhere to be seen. He was already able to walk, and was probably down in therapy right then. Thomas was up and about more than ever, while Tabetha, over the course of these last few days, found that even getting around in her wheelchair had become a struggle.

Tabetha heard nurses' voices in the hall, just outside her room. They were talking to someone, a visitor ... her mother, she realized with a thrill, and heaved herself forward in bed. Like a crocus pushing up through the last crust of snow, Tabetha's smile broke wide and free as her mother stepped through the doorway, a red tin of cookies pressed between her hands.

"Mom!"

Tabetha's mother kissed her forehead, gave her an extra long hug and then sat down nervously at the edge of her bed.

She had been crying. Tabetha could tell.

Her mother smiled, but in that too-big way, and Tabetha

wondered what could make her mother sad on a day such as this, a day when the two of them could be together.

To cheer her up, Tabetha hefted the oval fishbowl from her bedstand to her lap. The water inside sloshed around from the movement. "Look, Mom, the salamanders are growing! They only just hatched and this one here is already as big as my finger. Look how yellow it is!"

The second of the two salamanders curled behind a screen of twisted driftwood at the bottom of the fishbowl. Tabetha turned the glass bowl around so her mother could see. "And this one here is blue. *Really* blue, and just look at them!"

Her mother blinked in surprise. She leaned closer. "Honey, are those really . . ." She straightened, the look of shock plain on her face. "I don't know much about salamanders, but they're like, strange, Tab. Really strange."

"They're pretty, huh."

Her mother just frowned. "Let me see that yellow one again." Tabetha turned the bowl back around, her mother's face leaning in close to the glass. "My god," her mother murmured to herself. "I had no idea they had colors like that. Is that normal? They're like . . . it's like they're glowing."

With the salamanders between them, Tabetha saw her mother's amazed face through the glass, sort of stretched and warping around the bend of the bowl. Suddenly her mother sat up tall and met Tabetha's eyes. "Who gave them to you again?"

Uh-oh.

Tabetha looked away. She had hoped her mother wouldn't

ask. Of course she could just tell her mother how she had found them, and that they were not just salamanders but keys, and that Tabetha needed them to unlock the magic of the pyramids and retrieve the remaining two Puzzle Beads so that an evil sorcerer who actually slept in that bed right over there would not find them first and fit the beads together and destroy the Hedge that protected the Earth from the evils of the universe.

But Tabetha suspected this was not the thing to do. Her mother would probably want to know more, and Tabetha had no desire to tell it. So she decided on a much simpler version of the truth.

"Someone's salamander laid eggs and died."

Her mother scowled. After a long pause, she went, "Hmmph," and jounced her eyebrows and shook her head, seemingly satisfied that children could be at once baffling and cute.

Then, without warning, her mother fell quiet, staring fixedly into the palms of her hands. Tabetha worried for her and these dark shifts of mood. After a loud, slow exhale, her mother willfully brightened, slapped her thighs gently and took the glass bowl from Tabetha's hands. She returned it to the bedstand, picked up the red tin of cookies she'd brought and pushed it into Tabetha's arms.

"Extra Big Double Chocolate Chip, your favorite kind," she said with a quick sniff, and though she smiled again, that deep sadness hadn't yet left her eyes, now glistening as if freshly painted.

Tabetha glanced down at the cookie tin. She muttered a

thank you and slowly dragged a finger back and forth across the lid. Without looking up, she asked, "Mom, when am I going home?"

Her mother said nothing for a long time, as if paralyzed by the question. Her voice quaked faintly when she spoke. "It's not that simple, Tab."

"But Thomas is already walking. He doesn't even need crutches anymore. When am I going to get better?"

Tabetha looked up. Her mother's lips were pinched tight, her chin quivering uncontrollably. Tabetha felt a sharp ache growing in her chest.

"Mommy?"

Her mother's tears broke loose. She pressed a trembling hand to her mouth. "I don't . . . I don't think it's going to happen, honey."

"But . . ."

Her mother shook her head, sobbing freely now. "I'm so sorry, Tabetha. I'm so, so sorry." She kissed Tabetha's head, wrapped her fiercely in her arms. Her mother's whisper felt like steam in her hair.

"The doctors say you're going to die, Tabetha."

$$\mathcal{L}$$

Alas, I needn't tell you how lonely a child feels, struggling to understand matters that overwhelm most adults. When a mother breaks down, when she can no longer form words through the tears, how is a child to find meaning in her own passage?

I do not know.

I do not know and for this reason my hand trembles to write these words.

All that day and into the night, Tabetha lay in her bed. Thinking. After her mother had left, Tabetha spent hours watching the drip-drip of the IV, her mind chasing down thought after thought as if any one of them might be her hero in disguise. Yet every thought led to the same place. The place all things finish.

The end. It grieves me to say so, but Tabetha's short life was ending, and no amount of thinking could push it back. The light through the window went from yellow to orange. The noise in the hallway trickled to a mutter. Tabetha barely noticed.

Only when the violet of evening washed across the hospital walls and Thomas finally returned on slippered feet, only then did Tabetha snap alert from her brooding. Thomas had been gone all day, except he hadn't been downstairs in physical therapy. Not all that time. Tabetha didn't need to ask where he'd gone.

In the cool darkness of her room, Tabetha rolled to her side and silently watched Thomas climb into his bed. He'd been in Wrush. She knew because he went every day now.

While she had been cautious, careful not to waste any ink, Thomas had grown feverish in his use of his magic pen. He wrote his way to Wrush at all hours of the day, even skipping noon medicine to journey.

Tabetha, on the other hand, hadn't returned once since finding the first pyramid. With the magic ink of their pens running out, she was waiting for her salamanders to grow up, refusing to leave until they were ready.

Thomas lay awake beside his window, black hair tousled and glistening, hands tucked behind his head. Despite his hurried adventures, Tabetha had noticed a change in the boy. A change that was growing more and more obvious.

Before, Thomas had glared and snorted like some hateful beast in a cage. But now his unkindness seemed limited to silence. He avoided her eyes, as if the threat of guilt was hidden there, and once, to Tabetha's complete surprise, he secretly presented an extra pen cap to replace one she had lost. All in all, Thomas seemed less an angry boy than a sad one, spending long thoughtful hours before the window. There were even times when Tabetha felt certain he was ashamed, perhaps wishing to give up his selfishness and cruelty but no longer remembering how.

Yes, she decided as she watched him now, Thomas was definitely different. Sadder. The red-hot coals of his anger had cooled. But then why so many journeys back to Wrush? Thomas had a copy of the Pyramid Map, just like herself. Was the second pyramid so very hard to find?

She flipped her pillow over, felt the coolness against her cheek. She smelled ammonia from the hall where they mopped. Tabetha thought about the Pump Dragons, her mother, how she might say good-bye to her friends. So much goodness here in life she'd leave behind. She wondered what it was like when people died, where they went and how they fared, and was suddenly struck with the most peculiar feeling.

It was all okay.

Everything.

Somehow, she knew there was nothing to fear.

Of course it made no sense; she should be shaking with dread. But have you, dear reader, ever felt that warm glow deep within? That little flame that makes everything all right? If you have, do not ever ignore it. It is the treasure no one can ever take away.

"I love them! . . .
What are they?"

*L*ate that night, when it seemed all the world slept and only Tabetha could hear its secret murmur, she made her decision. She literally had no time to lose. If they were not yet fully grown, the salamanders had hatched at least, and however big they were would have to do.

She was going to Wrush, tonight, right now, and nothing was large enough or terrible enough or strong enough to stop her. The warm glow in her belly only grew brighter with this decision and Tabetha, for the briefest of instants, actually had a sense of the world turning, and herself resting atop it, knowing that whatever happened this— *this glow*— would be forever and always.

In a particularly brave moment, Tabetha pulled back the sticky tape from her arm. She slid the IV catheter out. A tiny red bead of blood appeared, and she covered it with an old band-aid from her elbow. She removed the salamanders from their tank, each impossibly bright, and along with her jar of frowns, she slipped them all into the left and right pockets of her pajamas.

There were no longer thoughts of getting caught, nor fears of being missed. There was only that warm glow in her belly, and she was leaving. Without bothering to pull the curtains about her bed for privacy, Tabetha tugged her magic pen from its hiding place beneath the mattress. She took sheets of paper from the drawer, and by the faint light of the moon, began to write what would soon become known as her last and greatest journey of them all.

But let us pause for a moment. Let us savor this image. Allow me to paint a last picture in your mind: Tabetha, her face as clear as spring rain, in her final moments before departing our world.

I have always enjoyed this image, the calm cast of her eyes. It pleases me to remember her this way. I see her gazing down upon her paper, something unnamable in the air, her magic pen like a bolt of lightning in her hand. The room is dim. There is a bar of moonlight on the floor. The only sound is the sound of her breathing.

I see her shaking the pen, just a few times for encouragement. I see her lower its fine tip to the page. And then the first scritch— the sound of ink as it flows— that smallest sound that rips the roof off of night.

Amidst thunder and howling wind, Tabetha poured herself into her story. Her hair whipped about her face as she wrote. The scent of ink rose up thick as incense from her pen and it smelled not of this world, but others. Tabetha scrawled a short phrase and smelled the crisp air of a palace. She added details and smelled a candle's perfume.

The wind about her fell away. The thunder grew quiet. The words of her story blurred clean off the pages until the velvety lights of a distant land swirled about her. Tabetha set down her pen.

In Wrush.

The tiles of the Citadel were cool beneath her skin, the entire palace made of fossilized cloud. Pigeon coos echoed from airy domes. Tabetha sat in the center of the Great Hall, her blue pajamas unruffled, the empress's throne directly ahead. She glanced around, quieted, much aware that something was different.

The hollow elegance of the Citadel was unchanged, the walls still blazing with countless candles. But Tabetha's old hesitations, her shyness and anxiety, all those feelings that had long gripped her were uncoiling. She could almost watch them come free, like a knot or a braid, watch them sail high as a kite without string.

She brought a hand to her head and felt the Orchid Crown there. The Citadel's tiles were white as gleaming bones. She closed her eyes.

"Ahoy there!" came the familiar cry, and Tabetha blinked at the doors as they opened just wide enough to admit the Mungling. He was blazing with joy as he rushed right passed her and sat himself down.

On a swing. He sat himself down on a swing.

"Tabetha, you must give this a try!"

Amazingly, amid the brilliance of her arrival, Tabetha had failed to notice the swings. They hung in two parallel lines, seemingly fixed in midair, along opposite walls of the Great Hall. She had always thought the place could use a bit of furniture.

"Now watch this!" cried the Mungling from the swing, pumping all six of his limbs and careening dangerously over her head. He was very high.

"Wahoo!" At the summit of his arc, the Mungling threw himself free of the swing and tucked into an acrobatic ball. He spun three or four times, perhaps fifty feet in the air, then *poofed!* into a cloud of dazzling white powder.

Tabetha was astonished. She watched wide-eyed as the powder drifted down to the floor, where it clotted and thickened back into the Mungling. He stood there on the white tiles before her, delighted and completely unharmed.

"Not bad, huh? You like them?"

"I love them!" she said. "What are they?"

"Powder Swings. Answer thought a few chairs might warm the place up a bit. I suggested a water slide. He said some magic carpets might do the trick, and next thing we knew, we we're talking swings. Except Answer wanted them to be safe for you, of course, so he set them up so nobody could fall. Jump from any height, Tabetha, any height at all, and the worst that will happen is a sneeze."

The Mungling embraced her, his skin flashing like a firefly in his excitement. "Tabetha," he said, squeezing tighter. "So glad you're back. You look . . ." He paused, leaning back for a glance. For the briefest instant, concern flickered in his eyes, his smile going loose at the corners. Then his face lit with joy once again, and he pulled her back to his chest. "You look great, Tabetha," he whispered. "It's wonderful to see you."

With the spindly arms of her best friend about her shoulders, Tabetha felt a sudden sadness open up, like discovering an empty nest in her chest. She knew the Mungling felt it too, though he pretended he didn't. Not long from now, they would be saying good-bye. Perhaps for the very last time.

"You know," he said, the old sparkle returning to his voice. "Answer and I argued for nearly three days over the color."

"The color?" She wrinkled her nose. "Of what?"

"The powder, Tabetha. What color powder you'd poof into each time you jump from the swings!"

"I think the white is very nice."

"Of course it is. I insisted upon it. Answer wanted rain colors and invisible colors and colors turned inside out. Wizardish stuff, you know. But I said white. Keep it simple, I said. You know me. Not too picky, so long as I get what I want."

"Well I like it," she assured him.

"You ready for a try?"

Tabetha hesitated. The thrill of arrival was already giving way to fatigue. Like sand slipping through a hole in a sack, her body's strength was leaving her, even as she spoke. "I think not right now," she said politely, silently wondering if there would be another chance. Then a thought occurred to her, both frightening and abrupt. She had made a promise once to the Mungling and she hadn't yet seen it through.

"Mungling," she said. "About your name. I think maybe it's time we start looking."

"No worries, Tabetha." He waved two of his six hands in the air. "That's not what's important right now."

"But I made you a promise. And I don't . . . I'm not too sure how much longer we have." By the sadness in his eyes, she saw that the Mungling understood.

"Later," was all he said. "For now, there's something you have to see. Remember how the Pyramid Map changed when we arrived in Tsepudra?"

"Uh huh." She recalled how the landscape of the map shifted depending on where the Mungling was.

"Well," the Mungling said, eagerly rubbing four of his hands. "The Map changed again the moment we returned to Wrush. It shows completely different landmarks now. Answer has been studying it and thinks he's found the second pyramid." The Mungling paused. "There's just one little thing."

"What's that?" asked Tabetha, and the Mungling grinned.

"The only way to the second pyramid is by Wink Hole!"

And you must wonder, dear reader, at a time such as this, how a word like *hole* can mean "nothing," as well as "everything at once," with the addition of a W being the only difference. For a W, after all, has no real notion of space, and is only two V's linked together arm in arm.

Now V is a letter that should not be ignored. Turned on its side, it points you in a direction. But in Wrush, unfortunately, there is no such thing as a V, nor has there ever been a word for *direction*.

"Where are we going?" Tabetha asked after the Mungling helped her onto his back and secured her in his leather saddle. He carried her through a small passage at the back of the Great Hall and down several narrow, glittering corridors until it became apparent they were completely lost.

Tabetha asked again and the Mungling replied, "Oh, we're going this way and that. It's all the same really, so long as we arrive where we're headed."

"But I don't know where we're headed."

"To see Answer," said the Mungling. "He'll be in the Observatory, no doubt. I haven't been able to pull him away since you left."

The sun-wyrm continued along more halls that all looked very much the same, muttering strange formulas to himself, such as: *Well, two wrongs don't make a right, but three lefts surely do.* He would turn according to his logic and begin mumbling his nonsense again, all the while picking his way through the labyrinth.

Tabetha didn't mind. "Well, I've brought something with me that might grab Answer's attention." She patted the pockets of her pajamas, feeling the soft movement of her salamanders inside. "Two things, actually." Then she began humming to herself in a distracted way, her eyes roaming her surroundings. It occurred to Tabetha that all this was hers. Everything. This empire, this city, this palace, and its maze. As empress, she'd never even had time to explore it.

"What's Answer observing, anyway?" she asked as they neared the Observatory entrance. "Stars?" As far as she knew, that's what observatories were for.

The Mungling shook his head. "Dust," he said. "Answer's studying dust. He's not just the High Wizard of Wrush, you know, but an initiate. A Dustonomer of the highest order."

"A Dustonomer? I never heard of that job."

"Oh yes. The science of Dustonomy is highly regarded. Dangerous though. Much riskier than astronomy. Wizards only attempt it after mastering all else, for many a wise man has gone mad trying to understand the true nature of dust. In fact long ago, long before Answer, there was a High Wizard who called himself Ee Aaia. Lost his mind completely, poor man. Spent the last of his days eating crayons and trying to count to ten on his thumbs."

At that moment, the corridor widened into a doorless entranceway. They crossed the threshold and entered an enormous chamber, as silent and imposing as the rest.

The Observatory.

Its ceiling was high and shaped like an overturned bowl. The floor was sunken like an amphitheater. All across the broad dome, Tabetha saw tiny sparkles, dust particles blinking in the light. This chamber looked just like a star observatory, but for *dust*!

"Tabetha!" said the wizard with a wave of his hand. She glanced down the many steps to the circular platform at the center of the room. Her eyes found Answer climbing from the seat of the most bizarre contraption. "Tabetha, you must come down here!" he shouted. "I've been aching to show you this!"

The Mungling carried her down the steps to greet the High Wizard. As she neared him, the air in the Observatory became sharp and alive. It was as if an invisible cloud of excitement hung about the boy. As he hugged her, she felt the shelter of his arms, and in his voice was all the protective warmth of a brother.

"You know, Tabetha," he said, suddenly transformed by the moment. "We've come through a lot, you and I. It seems so long ago, that day we first met. And in some ways, nothing has changed. You're the empress; I'm still your wizard. Yet when I saw you just now, at the top of those steps, I swear I had to remind myself you're the same girl."

"What do you mean?" she asked against his chest.

"I mean," he said, "that you're different. You've grown. Something that was only a seed in you has become like a tree. It's enough to steal the breath out of wind."

"I think I kind of understand," she said. "Something changed inside before I left for Wrush. I could feel it, and can feel it changing still."

"Like a tree," he said.

She nodded faintly. "Like a tree."

Suddenly Tabetha had a clear image of this tree, reaching and branching with all the force of spring growth. It stretched up through her heart and climbed the skies of her mind, and then the wizard smiled, and she knew he saw it too, for these pictures in her head were his doing.

"Now," he said in a voice that drew her back to this room. "Now for that special something I wished to show you." Answer turned to the many knobs and meters of his extravagant machine. She realized it was nothing more than a telescope, an enormous one, its long tubular lens cranked skyward like a canon. It had hundreds of dials and polished levers galore, but the strangest part about it was the shape. The shape was all wrong.

"Aren't you supposed to look through the skinny end of a telescope, with the wide part at the end?" she asked, for that's how it was when her father set up his telescope on the lawn each summer. Answer's contraption was like staring into the wrong end of a trumpet.

"You're thinking of a telescope," Answer replied, "which is a wonderful tool. Very useful when you want to see far away things up close. But this here is a Dustonomer's Scope." He patted the flaring barrel of it. "It makes close-up things appear far."

"What use is that?" asked Tabetha, knowing from the wizard's grin she was about to find out.

For explanation, Answer pointed to a single speck of dust high in the air. It floated with countless others beneath the crystal dome, and the way light cut across them, Tabetha could have believed she was staring up into space, witnessing a million billion stars flung about the soft twirls of a galaxy.

"Do you see it, that one there?" Answer waggled his finger at the ceiling. "That little flicker is none other than Mote 716-G. Otherwise known as Arctus Ulai, the seventh-largest Mote in the universe.

"Mote?" she repeated. "What's a Mote?"

"A Dust Star," he explained. "Here, take a seat and have a look for yourself." Answer lifted her from the Mungling's saddle and placed her before the viewing glass at the wide end of the Dustonomer's Scope.

"Just . . . look into it?" she asked, and the wizard nodded eagerly.

Tabetha brought her small face up to the glass, expecting to see that same fleck of dust, except maybe bigger or closer. What she found, however, was like the surprise you might feel when picking up a pinecone, only to realize a whole forest lies hidden within.

"That dream, it is an old one. Many have had it before you."

*D*ust Stars.

That's what she saw. Peering into the Dustonomer's Scope, Tabetha found a night sky come alive, a screen of comets and bright things pulsing.

"Dust," she heard the wizard say, as though from afar. "Everything you see there is dust."

Her eyes glued to the eyepiece, she said, "But they look like worlds. Countless worlds all spinning about. If that's what dust really looks like, if that's what dust really is, that means . . ."

"It means the universe is big, Tabetha. Really big."

Answer adjusted the scope and Tabetha saw something like a planet of pure ice drop into view. It was different from the others, in a way she couldn't describe. "What's that?" she asked with a shrinking feeling inside.

Answer dipped his head for a glance through the scope. "That's it, Tabetha, Arctus Ulai. That's where the second pyramid is hidden."

"You're sure?"

"It's all right here," replied the Mungling, tapping the map on the back of his head. "Answer's the one who figured it out, of course. At first he didn't even know what all these strange marks were. Then he realized I've got a map of dust Motes right here, every one of them, and he's been hunkering over that darn scope ever since."

"Well, at least this Arctus Ulai is nearby," said Tabetha, not yet bothering to wonder how she might fit upon a Mote. "At least we can see it from here."

The wizard heaved a sigh. "Actually, it's far, Tabetha. Farther than any star you might see in the sky."

Tabetha pointed in confusion. "But it's only right there."

"Trust me, Tabetha. You'll have to trust me on this one. It is far. Very, very far. The Dustonomer's Scope only puts Motes into their true perspective. I know it's puzzling, but it's the puzzle of it that keeps you safe. Those who insist on understanding scorch their minds."

Tabetha nodded, feeling rather glad to have a wizard.

"The important thing is we know how to get there," Answer added, and the Mungling let out a jubilant chirp. "The Wink Hole!" he cried. "Just like I told you! There's a Wink Hole that goes straight to Arctus Ulai!"

"Where?" Tabetha asked, a sudden thrill prickling her skin. "Where is this new Wink Hole?"

Answer then removed a folded note from a pouch at his side. "This came for you," he said, "some time ago. I hope you don't mind, but I read it."

"For me?" she said, receiving the creased page. "But what does this have to do with the Wink Hole? And who would even write me a note?"

"You are the empress, you know. You've already made quite a name for yourself. That isn't a note you hold, but an invitation. It seems you made an impression on some Grimpkins once. Grimpkins who now cordially invite Her Majesty Tabetha Bright the First for a cup of tea."

Tabetha opened up the invitation and scanned it halfway. "I hope you told them no," she said, recalling the Grimpkins' magical pranks, their treacherous thirst for laughter.

"Actually I told them yes," Answer replied.

"Yes?" Tabetha was baffled. "Why would you do that?"

The wizard's finger drew her attention to a single, coiling symbol upon the map. "Because the Wink Hole we seek is here," he said, and as if pushing a button, the tiny black spiral began to spin at his touch.

"Here. In the very heart of Grimpkin's Hollow."

So it appeared that Tabetha and her friends were headed back to Grimpkin's Hollow to find the Wink Hole to Arctus Ulai. They had only begun discussing the matter when a booming voice interrupted them with these dreaded words:

"Morlac is here!"

This cry of alarm seemed to come from everywhere at once, such was the bounce of echoes in the Observatory. All present turned as one to find Isaac, his eager bulk panting in the entranceway. His massive chest heaved as though he'd been running hard, his thick beard and blue tunic damp with sweat.

"Here?" Tabetha called back, already mounting her saddle. "Thomas Morlac is here, in the floating city of Etherios?"

Isaac hitched his long sword further back on his hip, his black boots clicking loudly as he rushed down the steps. "No, My Lady, here!" he cried. "In the Citadel!"

Tabetha was astonished, but before she could speak, her wizard's voice arced over her shoulder. "Is Morlac alone?" Answer called out. "Like last time?"

Like last time? What was Answer talking about? Thomas Morlac had never been to the Citadel before.

"Morlac is not alone," Isaac replied, coming to an abrupt halt before them. "He brings ten Gwybies in escort. They await you, My Lady, all of them, in the Citadel's Great Hall."

Not long ago, this news might have stricken her. There was a time when it would've knocked the air from her lungs. But not now. Fatigue draped her body like a gown of chains, yet Tabetha could still feel that warm glow deep within. A glow that throbbed through her limbs like lit courage.

"I'm ready," she said. "More than ever before. Tell Thomas the empress will gladly see him."

It is not possible for me to explain just how much one girl can grow, how much she can change in order to meet a great challenge. I will say this, however: The warm glow inside Tabetha had become a thing alive. It breathed and it pulsed and matured.

Isaac rushed ahead, carrying her words to the dark sorcerer. Tabetha rode the Mungling with the boy-wizard at her side. "Are you sure this is safe?" asked the Mungling, his concern undisguised. "You've never had a confrontation quite like this. What if it's a trap?"

Tabetha felt very quiet inside. She said, "I don't think Thomas means to harm me. Don't ask me why."

She turned to Answer. "What did you mean by 'last time'? When you asked Isaac about last time, you made it sound like Thomas Morlac had been here before."

The wizard nodded slowly, his ink-dark eyes flashing with some memory. "He has been here," Answer replied. "Once."

Tabetha halted the Mungling.

"Thomas came here," her wizard continued, "when I was still his teacher."

"His teacher?"

Answer nodded, explaining, "When Thomas first discovered Wrush, he came as you did Tabetha: a child stunned by the weight of wonder. There was something magnificent in the air about him, as though he had an important role to play. Thinking he might be the one, the child meant to free all worlds from darkness, I began teaching Thomas the secrets of magic. He learned quickly, and in no time had mastered the arts. But his skill soon overshadowed his heart. His power was too great, and his anger soon festered, so when he asked for the throne I denied him."

"The throne? You mean Thomas was to be emperor of Wrush?"

"If I had allowed it, yes."

"Then you stopped him," said Tabetha. "You kept the empire from harm."

"Yes," said Answer. "And no. When he came for the throne I stopped him. I knew his heart wasn't pure, and the throne's magic would destroy him. When Thomas insisted, I cast a spell to prevent him."

"Then you saved Thomas," she said. "You saved him from turning himself to stone."

The boy-wizard nodded solemnly at the memory. "The spell I cast did that and more," he went on. "It kept Thomas from taking the throne, but also trapped me. It locked me away until a true leader appeared, the child who would set me free, and so prove her worth to the empire."

"The Ovidium," Tabetha murmured, remembering the strange magic mirror she had encountered on her first trip to Wrush. "You made the Ovidium. You locked yourself within, to keep Wrush safe from Morlac."

"Until you came," he said. "Yes. But by that time, Thomas had already learned to create monsters. His Gwybies followed his every command."

"They tore down the last of the Noble Trees," the Mungling added, "driving the Pump Dragons from Wrush. To this day they still tunnel through the universe and weep."

For their fruit, thought Tabetha. *They tunnel in search of their Noble Trees.* Upon this thought, her mind fell away and was replaced by a familiar image.

Her dream . . . the blue hill from her dream.

As so often happened when she heard mention of the Pump Dragons, Tabetha's old dream came alive. But this time, it was stronger than ever. To the wizard she appeared lost in a trance.

She wandered across the field that stretched behind her old house, the sky above an impossible blue. It was quiet. Sparkling. No one around.

She ran through mixed grasses, so tall they slapped at her chest, her eyes fixed on the hill beyond the fence-line. It swelled lonely and grand, carpeted in tiny blue flowers. Forget-me-nots, she thought they were called. The flowers grew so thick that from a distance they were one, making the hill appear like a giant half-buried plum.

She climbed it, feeling the sun on her cheeks. She lay down upon the summit and wept. It was always like this. Blue flowers, blue sky. Tears without sadness. And she was not alone. And this hill was her home. Only when she shut her eyes did she wake.

"Tabetha!" whispered the Mungling. "Tabetha, are you all right?"

Slowly, she came to her senses. She blinked into her surroundings— the corridor, the faces— still blurred by her memory of the hill. What that dream was about, she had yet to understand, but if it got any stronger she believed it might sweep her away.

"I'm fine," she assured him. "It was just my dream again. Every time you speak of Pump Dragons, Mungling, I start to—"

She stopped, realizing what she said. It was only when the

Mungling spoke of Pump Dragons that this dream came alive. As though his voice could call upon them like a bell. What was it about him? About Pump Dragons and her hill? And why did thoughts of their Noble Trees make her eyes sting?

The wizard took her pulse, checked the whites of her eyes. "That dream," he said. "It is an old one. Many have had it before you. But it's different now. It's different for you, and I can't say I understand why. My sense is that it has something to do with Earth— with the fact that you're from there." He asked her to follow the movement of his finger without moving her head, and then nodded with satisfaction. "I don't know why that dream affects you as it does, Tabetha, but you appear fine now. Do you feel well enough to keep on?"

Tabetha remembered Morlac, waiting for her in the Great Hall. She forced all her questions aside. "I do," she said, and urged the Mungling on.

Moments later, the white corridor narrowed, and sounds from further ahead began to swell. They grew louder and louder the closer she approached, then fell suddenly silent as Tabetha and her friends entered the Great Hall.

There was Thomas Morlac, just as Isaac had said. The evil sorcerer right here in her hall. He stood tall for a boy his age, no sign of any illness about him. He awaited Tabetha with ten of his Gwybies. Which she smelled.

Morlac's eyes appeared nervous as Answer and the Mungling helped Tabetha onto her throne. Her friends took up positions to her left and right, while Isaac stood tall and fearsome just behind. With surprising elegance, the great warrior bent over her shoulder to adjust the Orchid Crown upon her head, whispering, "Morlac tells me nothing of his purpose, My Lady, except that he wishes to see you."

Tabetha nodded, and in the clear voice of an empress, invited her new guest and his Gwybies to make themselves comfortable. To take seats.

Reluctantly at first, the Gwybies looked about the enormous room, eyeing the magic swings that hung slack and irresistible. Though Thomas Morlac frowned in disapproval, and remained standing himself, his creatures cautiously took up their seats.

And to everyone's surprise, they began to swing.

Just idle kicks, of course. Nothing too childish, but Tabetha was delighted all the same. Peering closer, it seemed she glimpsed *joy* in the faces of those hideous beasts, even laughter behind their brightening eyes.

Thomas Morlac became all the more dismayed at their behavior, obviously wishing to appear terrible and dignified.

Nonetheless, he stepped toward the throne, clearing his throat before speaking.

"Tabetha," he said evenly, clearly avoiding the gaze of his old teacher. "You're probably wondering why I'm here."

"Well, yeah," she confessed.

He swallowed, his eyes flicking to Answer and then back to her. "It's not to surrender. Or apologize, if that's what you're thinking."

She said nothing.

"I'm here because . . ." He cleared his throat again, this time more harshly. "I'm here because I need something. Something from you."

Now this she hadn't expected. Thomas couldn't possibly know that her pockets held the Wrushic Salamanders he needed, or that the first Puzzle Bead was tucked beneath the collar of her pajamas. This surprised her because it was so unlike Thomas to admit need of anything. Yes, he was definitely changing. Definitely.

The question was, *into what.*

At this moment, Thomas Morlac held up a sheet of paper, the original Pyramid Map he'd taken from her in Haza Mugad. "The map is flawed," he announced. "You already know that, as you're the one who ruined it. But your Pepper Spit did more damage than you probably realize. Even though I know the second pyramid lies hidden in Arctus Ulai— I can see that much clearly— the Wink Hole to Arctus Ulai remains a mystery to me."

So that's why Thomas had been rushing back and forth to Wrush. He knew where the second pyramid was, but had no idea how to get there.

"So you've been searching for the right Wink Hole?" Tabetha asked, and he nodded.

"Everywhere," he said. "I've tried every Wink Hole I know of, but none take me to Arctus Ulai."

Tabetha looked at him now, her hospital roommate, a crippled boy who could suddenly walk. In that instant, she realized that even if Thomas Morlac failed to tear down the Hedge and conquer all with his Gwybies, her world would be no closer to peace. She envisioned Earth with its pollution and its wars, its hatred and its crime. Images flickered through her mind. She saw vast stretches of forest, now blackened and torn. Filthy cities belched smog from black stacks. She saw children begging on the streets, and grim-faced soldiers waving guns. This was Earth now, even before Thomas's invasion.

Out of nowhere, like the hatch in a warplane, a door opened in the floor of Tabetha's mind and a steady stream of bombs poured out, one after another. They plunged toward Earth, whistling louder and louder. The ground approached at incredible speed. That's when Tabetha understood that she was falling too— had been falling from the start. That the world would shake when she landed and would never be the same. That she was, in her own way, the last bomb.

Tabetha looked to Thomas, the glow in her belly leaping up through her heart. With a jolt, she understood what she had to do.

"I'll show you the map," she said.

"What?" the Mungling squawked, but Answer silenced him with a heavy glance.

"I'll let you see the Pyramid Map, Thomas," she repeated, "but on one condition."

Tabetha had a task. She had a duty, so unusual and great, it went far beyond the map, or Thomas, or anything that might happen in this room. A task that rocked her with the full force of its meaning.

"A condition?" Thomas snorted, but he seemed more amused than dismayed. "All right then, tell me what you want in exchange."

Her attention went briefly to the Gwybies, who had finally discovered the magic of the swings. They leapt with unconcealed joy, combusting into the clouds of white powder that now hazed the Great Hall.

"Promise me this," said Tabetha. "Promise that if I manage to get to all three pyramids before you . . . you'll change."

"Change?" Thomas shifted from one foot to the other. "What do you mean, change?"

"I mean you'll be a different person. You'll go back to the person Answer says you once were."

Upon saying these words, she could almost feel the crack that opened up in Thomas's heart.

"I want you to promise me that if you fail, Thomas, you'll start being kind to other people."

That crack grew wider, and she could almost feel herself spilling through.

"I want you to be kind to yourself."

And then she was in. And he'd never get her back out.

Thomas's face went slack. His eyes took on a faraway look. Even before he spoke, Tabetha knew what he'd say.

"Okay," he agreed simply, in a voice unlike ever before.

Tabetha whispered to the Mungling, who started down the steps toward Thomas.

"You and the Mungling can meet out in the courtyard," she said aloud. "He'll show you the Pyramid Map. Take as long as you need. But I want you to wait one hour before setting off for the Wink Hole. Since you can walk on your own, and I still can't, it's only fair. And there's something you should know about where you're going, about the Grimpkins."

"No more Tabetha," he cut her off abruptly. "I said I promised, and I mean to keep it. That's enough."

"But—" Tabetha started, wanting to give him fair warning, but he would hear nothing of it. He turned from her, gathering his Gwybies with a sharp gesture. He headed for the twin doors at the far end of the hall, and then paused unexpectedly at the threshold. He did not turn around. Head hunched, as though caught up in some secret struggle, his voice was soft and low when it reached her.

"I hear it's cold in Arctus Ulai," he said, then paused, his head coming up. "You should probably bring something warm." And then he was through the twin doors, the immense light of day blotting his form.

She heard the slow scrape of Isaac drawing his sword.

O don't know what just happened," said Isaac, his eyes bright with awe. "Nor will I ever forget it. Whatever passed between you and Morlac just now is unheard of, My Lady. He actually listened to you."

Tabetha felt her legs cramping on the throne, then Answer's hand upon her shoulder. "More than that, Tabetha. Morlac was almost kind. You did great, just like an empress." Her wizard smiled, and then leaned down and kissed the top of her head, just like her mother— and then her mother's last words crashed in.

I'm so sorry, Tabetha. I'm so, so sorry.

The doctors, they say . . .

Tabetha's pulse quickened. An ache swelled in her throat. She tried to swallow it back but it thickened. Then the Mungling returned, having finished showing Morlac the map. The sun-wyrm took up a seat on the steps below her.

"Tabetha," he began, and then swallowed. There was the slightest quaver in his voice. "Tabetha, I know you do everything for a reason. And I've been stuck here in Wrush so long, unable to return home without my name, that until I met you, I thought life was just a heap of obstacles."

"Obstacles?" she repeated, for though she may have been an empress and the universe's last hope, the defiant champion of our troubled age, Tabetha, I must remind you, had not yet reached the fifth grade. "What are obstacles?" she asked.

"Well that's just the thing," the Mungling explained. "They're difficulties. They're challenges that get in our way. But you've shown me time and again that, really, there are no such things as obstacles. You've always managed to unmask them somehow, revealing the opportunities that lay just beneath.

"What I'm trying to say is, every challenge you face makes you bigger somehow, and I do hope one day to resemble you. Yet still, something is troubling me, and I have to ask . . ." He took a nervous breath. "I have to ask *why*, Tabetha. Why have me show Morlac the Pyramid Map when you could have kept it to yourself? Why take the risk? There's nothing selfish in keeping goodness from harm's way."

"You question the empress?" came Isaac's stout voice.

"Just tell me this, Tabetha," said the Mungling. "Do you have a plan? That's all I want to know. If you have a plan, just say so, and that will be enough for me."

"I have a plan," she said, struck once again by an image of that secret task before her. "I have a plan, and it goes far beyond Thomas and whatever happens in Grimpkin's Hollow."

The Mungling exhaled in relief. "Whew! I mean, I should have assumed as much all along, but a plan . . ." He shook his head. "This is terrific, Tabetha! Terrific news."

Then Answer's midnight eyes were before her, inquisitive and bright. He had a way of keeping one honest with a glance. "What more can you say?"

Tabetha hesitated. "A little, I suppose." Her gaze fell to the tiles. "Only . . . only I can't tell you everything just yet."

And to herself she said, *Because if you knew all that I planned, you would try to stop me.*

$\mathcal{C}$

They set out at once.

Tabetha, the Mungling, Answer, and Isaac climbed down the swinging rope ladder that dropped from the floating city of Etherios. The moment their feet slapped hard ground, the group immediately cut west through the high meadows of Wrill, tramping paths through the sway of high grasses. Tabetha lurched along in her saddle, explaining as best she could how they might get past the Grimpkins.

"Once again, you're brilliant!" praised the Mungling upon hearing the first part of her plan. "You're the coyote of underdogs! I should have known you were already one step ahead of Morlac."

Tabetha heaved a sigh. *If only they knew it all,* she thought, certain that no one, not even the High Wizard of Wrush, suspected her secret task in full. She squinted against the rich blue of sunlight, the breeze pulsing over fields. A dark line of trees smeared the horizon, and Tabetha tensed.

Grimpkin's Hollow. A deep woodland of trickery and magic.

As they neared the forest's long shadow, Answer paused the group. "I think it's time, Tabetha. Are you ready? Do you have them?"

Tabetha reached into her pocket and removed the jar of frowns. She carefully unscrewed the lid. After hauling them around for so long, it was great to finally put them to use.

"Each of you gets one frown," Answer explained, and then he reached into the jar and distributed them to Tabetha and her friends.

Tabetha squished her frown between thumb and forefinger listening to the rubbery, squeaky noise it made. "Weird," she whispered to herself. It was soft and cool, but also very much alive. She could feel the firmness of muscles twitching within. With her fingers, Tabetha attempted to force the lips into a smile but they refused to hold such a shape, and instantly drew back into a deep pout.

The Mungling dropped his frown, and it flopped about in the dirt like a fish, bouncing as high as his knees. He eventually managed to pin it with a foot and retrieved the strange item.

"Hold them close," Answer instructed the friends. "Once we enter the hollow and sit down for tea with the queen, *these,*" and at this, Answer raised his frown for emphasis, "are about all we'll have to keep Grimpkins from sucking our souls dry."

Within moments Tabetha and her friends were swallowed, like bats in the night, by the murk of Grimpkin's Hollow. The shadows of tremendous mushrooms overwhelmed them. The air grew dank. Tabetha looked to the Mungling, whose puffy face glowed green with anxious light. She recalled that first night they'd met, when they'd crept eagerly through these very woods. So many adventures they'd had, now coming to an end. She felt more determined than ever to help him.

I *must find his name*, she thought as she peered about the gloom. *Only his true name can return the Mungling to his home.*

Overhead, the caps of moist mushrooms hunched like twisted umbrellas. Green mosses boiled up from the ground. Amidst the dripping of water she heard the soft footsteps of her friends. Then a terrible cackle clawed the air.

Ah! Hah hah hah hah hah!

Grimpkins . . .

And very close. Their horrid laughter echoed off toadstools and Tabetha went still. Her heart thumped. A blue mist crawled over the ground. She saw something sprinting— a wild-haired blur mixing the shadows. And then she sensed something behind her. A second creature leapt among the caps.

"Don't panic," came the wizard's tense whisper. Tabetha heard the slow scrape of Isaac drawing his sword.

Then silence, broken only by the eerie patter of dripping.

Only the wizard's eyes moved when he spoke.

"They're here."

Think back, dear reader, all the way back to Book One, and you will recall that *Grimpkin* may as well be the Wrushic word for *deceit*. Grimpkins are fraudulent little creatures, ever scheming and sly. Tabetha put more trust in hungry weasels.

But Grimpkin magic is wily and very hard to resist, even when you are prepared for it. Tabetha knew the Grimpkins would do anything to make her laugh. She also knew why she couldn't, why she had to scowl at all costs, for once Grimpkins started a person laughing they would never stop, and the Grimpkins would drink up their souls.

"Do they really eat laughter?" she heard Isaac whisper into his thick beard. His eyes followed countless shapes through the shadows.

"They do," the boy-wizard replied. "They'll do whatever it takes to get it. Even a rock finds it hard to stay stone-faced among them, and that's why you must never—"

Ah! Hah hah hah hah hah!

That mad cackle again. Tabetha decided she was frightened.

On some unseen cue, Grimpkins, everywhere, sprang clear of the shadows, came bouncing from their holes like rabbits. They crowded about Tabetha, tiny men with wild white hair and bulging eyes that wobbled like a doll's.

"Tee hee! Hello!" they called in the silliest voices, their faces pinched in the silliest grins. "Come with us! Come with us!" they invited, tugging at her clothes. "We'll lay you on soft pillows stuffed to bursting with giggles. We'll dress you in gowns of guffaws!"

Tabetha closed her eyes, flexing every muscle in her face as if her whole life depended on a frown. Because somehow, just looking at a Grimpkin felt ticklish all over. Their magic bounced like bubbles in her chest.

"We'll have none of your trickery," came the wizard's calm voice. Tabetha cracked open one eye to find him pressing the magic frown to his mouth. He nodded at Tabetha to do the same.

Tabetha retrieved the frown from her pocket, then quickly cupped her hands around it to prevent the lips from flopping or bouncing from her grip. She pressed them to her mouth as Answer had done, and then experienced the strange sensation of her own lips twisting into a frown. The muscles in her face still fought for a smile, but simply could not break the frown's hold. Her mouth felt wooden and ridiculous, especially when she tried to speak, knowing that her grimace did not match the tone of her words.

"I think it's working," she pouted.

Answer turned to her with a snarl. "Even better than I'd hoped."

The Mungling's lips appeared unable to settle on one mood. They twisted and contorted into endless variations of displeasure— a sneer, a scoff, a scowl, a sob— until it was exhausting just to glance at him.

All the while, the Grimkins' jokes and laughter coiled round the friends like a trap.

"It's the empress!" they hooted in ticklish delight. "The Empress of Wrush has come for tea!"

Isaac, huge Isaac with his great barrel chest, fought to keep the ferocity in his voice while his lips betrayed him with whining cries like a baby, "Get back you villains! You treacherous elves! You'll find nothing here worth eating but steel!"

Grimpkins clutched at their bellies and rolled in the moss. Their laughter was a bottomless well. At last they dried their googly eyes and resumed their silly antics. From atop the skinny shoulders of another, a very fat Grimpkin declared, "Enough of your wit, or you'll have us drinking each other! Now come! Follow us, for the Queen of the Hollow is waiting!"

And here I shall pause to add a bit of history, as I believe it will shed light on what is to come. There was once, in Wrush, a nomadic people. This means they wandered all over the land. They were kings and queens and they lived in enormous pavilions, pitching palaces the way others pitch tents. But to the goodfolk of Wrush they were known as *Grim Kin*, for there was a sorrow about them and their ways.

Why these kings wandered is not entirely clear, and no one is quite sure why they grieved. Some say they were cursed, and they forever sought some lost joy. Others say the Grim Kin never had it. But this much is clear: At some point, the grim ones disappeared altogether. The old kings with their sadness and their enormous felt tents wandered clean off the maps of old Wrush. Though it is possible, quite possible, I say, the Grim Kin simply went back to where they had come from.

The path through the forest was winding and wet. Giant toad-stools, stretching overhead like a tarp, kept the moist woods in deep shade. The Grimpkins did not lead in the normal manner of guides, but instead swarmed about Tabetha like gnats. So busy were they in joking and tumbling and pulling pranks that they took little notice of the foul expressions contorting the faces of Tabetha and her friends.

"How are you, My Lady?" Isaac asked after a time, for she had clearly begun slumping in her saddle.

"I'm fine," she assured him. She tried to squirm upright, but her exhaustion was getting harder to disguise. Her legs were knotted wood, her arms tingly and numb. Worst of all, her breathing had once again become labored. She wondered silently if she had enough time, as if it were no longer measured by clocks and rising suns, but by the tick of warm breath in her lungs.

In.

Out.

In.

Out.

How many more shallow gulps were left to her?

Huge limestone boulders slid free from the mists, their shoulders shrouded in mossy capes. Animals called out with strange hoots. Echoes skipped through the fog. Hidden somewhere in this dank hollow was the Wink Hole.

Tabetha covered one eye, hoping to catch a glimpse, for that is the only way to see a Wink Hole and avoid falling in. But there was nothing to be seen except mushrooms upon mushrooms and moss thick on the ground, sometimes piling waist-high in drifts. Then a sudden break in the forest revealed a grotto.

"Oooooh," she heard the Mungling coo.

The grotto was rich and damp, perfumed by the mushrooms whose caps twined above like weird fingers. The air was cool. It smelled green and musty. Tremendous grey stones, carved long ago into faces, stood upright in a pond of silver water. Tabetha peered down at her reflection. She saw a tiredness in her eyes. And beneath her reflection she saw a light, as if some secret fire bloomed below, and she wondered what magic slept in this pool's watery depths.

Tabetha turned. Like a flock of pigeons bursting into flight, the Grimpkins suddenly scampered back into the forest. An eerie emptiness remained, the grotto unnaturally quiet. Despite the presence of her friends, Tabetha felt oddly alone. She began pondering whom this Queen of the Hollow might be when she noticed something very unusual about the pond.

"Look at that!" she said, pointing to some ripples on the surface, a group of rings spreading out like glistening halos. Another drop of water fell from the mushrooms above and more circles opened up on the water. "And over there," she pointed again. This time the Mungling saw it too.

"Faces!" he declared. "I saw the face of a king, right there on the surface of the water!"

It was true. Each time a droplet splashed from the mushrooms to the pond, the image of a face, dark-bearded and crowned, flashed as though in a watery mirror.

Answer nodded to himself, suddenly understanding. "Memories," he said. "Like old photos on water. These are memories of the wandering kings of Wrush."

"The Grim Kin?" asked Isaac. "The sad nomads of old? But why remember them here?"

"I believe this forest was once their home," replied Answer. "For this water is not a pond, I now realize, but a spring. The legendary Spring of Mirth. It's made from pure laughter and flows deeper than a sea. Somewhere in its depths dwells their queen."

"And the kings?"

"We know they left here once in search of joy, but could find none in our world. Disappointed and broken, transformed by their sorrow, it seems they have returned to these woods in the end."

"What a nasty end," said Isaac, turning to spit upon the ground. "I'd rather be sad and free than return to this puddle. What a rotten place to go extinct."

"Not extinct," replied Answer. "I said 'transformed by their sorrow.' I believe the Grim Kin are still among us."

"Then where?" argued Isaac, turning in place. "Where are these sad kings of old?" For Isaac did not yet understand. He didn't know that when a sadness grows great, too heavy to carry, people can sink beyond all recognition. So it was with these kings, now shriveled and mad.

"He means the Grimpkins, Isaac," Tabetha said at last. "The wandering kings have become the Grimpkins."

"And the queen is their maker, and their mistress too." Answer turned back to the water. "Her names change with the seasons, but I will speak not one of them aloud. It is enough that we call her Queen of the Hollow."

At the mention of her title, the silver waters broke. A woman, not at all like a Grimpkin, rose up from the deep. Her wet hair was white, reminding Tabetha of poured milk, and it fell across her shoulders in slick sheets.

A pair of Grimpkins surfaced on either side of this woman, standing knee deep in the water like servants. One held a wooden tray, upon which balanced five goblets. The other clutched an enormous twisting vase.

Tea, thought Tabetha. There was tea in that vase, the same wicked stuff she'd been warned about. Upon this thought, the queen met Tabetha's eyes and without glancing away extended one hand for her cup. Immediately the Grimpkin at her side bent to pour tea from his vase. The other Grimpkin caught the stream in a goblet. The queen sipped casually, reclining back in the mirrored water. At last she spoke.

"So you've met my children?"

The Grimpkins. She was speaking of the Grimpkins. "I have," said Tabetha, and the Queen of the Hollow grinned, purple flecks glinting in her eyes.

She took another sip. "Then you know they are dangerous, and perhaps a little bit mad. I never dreamed you would be foolish enough to accept my offer."

"Your offer?"

"The invitation I sent. Surely that's why you're here." The

woman chuckled, and Tabetha felt ice down her spine. "I am queen, yes," the woman went on. "Beautiful and cruel, soaking in my private spring. But some joys are greater than others." She narrowed her eyes. "I wish to drink the joy of an empress."

Tabetha gasped, and the air hurt her lungs. She felt the closeness of these woods hugging her skin.

"But first," the queen continued. "We must share a cup of tea, you and I. All of you. As my guests, I insist."

The Grimpkins poured tea for Tabetha and her friends. The wizard leaned down and whispered, "Whatever you do, Tabetha, don't take a sip. That stuff is so enchanted I can feel it from here."

From the side of her mouth, she whispered, "But what if I have to?"

"Don't!" hissed the wizard. "Unless you want to end up like a Grimpkin. Take one sip and that's what you'll become, chained by need to this pool forever."

Tabetha nodded faintly, felt that warm glow in her belly. The time had come for her to speak.

"Thank you for the invitation," Tabetha began. "But we haven't come for tea. We're only here in Grimpkin's Hollow to ask a favor."

"Ask *me*? A favor?" The queen's laughter was shrill. "But little empress, you'll never leave here alive. What makes you think I'll give you anything?"

"Because," replied Tabetha. "I'll offer you something better in return. Take us to your Wink Hole, and let us leave when we choose."

"And in exchange?" the queen demanded.

"In exchange," said Tabetha, "we'll give you an entire *army* of laughter to drink from."

"Yup!" he cried, and the two of them plunged into darkness.

The agreement was simple. It went something like this: Tabetha was to tell a story. If, by the time she had finished, the pure enchantment of that story did not summon an entire army to the Spring of Mirth, then she and her friends would drink the queen's tea. They would give up their souls for her feasting.

However . . .

If by some inconceivable magic or miracle of storytelling the young empress's tale *did* conjure an army by the time it was complete, then the queen's Grimpkins would lead Tabetha and her friends to the Wink Hole.

So it was all about tea, then; who would drink it and who would not. Since the brew had come to figure so heavily in their lives, it should not surprise you that tea inspired Tabetha's story. She named it "Cinnamon Tea," right there on the spot.

So began the tale:

Once upon a time, long long ago, there was a kingdom without a king or queen. There was only a princess who was kind-hearted and young but forbidden, by law, to rule until she married. The princess did not mind so much, as she had little interest in the throne. But in a neighboring realm there lived an evil sultan. This sultan was a devious man who wished to marry the princess, not for love, but so that he might gain her father's land and riches.

The people of her kingdom were greatly dismayed and so sought out the Blue Witch for aid. The Blue Witch was cunning as can be. Indeed, she was so clever, they say, she could slip between a fox and his shadow. So to the Blue Witch they cried, "Please! Please help us!" And they offered her gold to end their woes. "Find some way to keep our kingdom free of dread neighbors!"

But the princess had a secret. She told not even her maids. The secret was that she loved the stableboy. The stableboy was poor as a puddle, but he was so gentle with her horses that over time the princess found she adored him. Such was her affection that she would marry the boy if she could, but first she had to make him love her.

Now the stableboy, too, had a secret of his own. His secret involved the princess's gold. He wanted it, just like the sultan, and had a plan fixed in his mind. He would woo the princess with kindness and be such a charming fellow as to make her desire him for her husband and throne.

So it was that each of them, the princess and the stableboy, set out alone for the Blue Witch with the hope of acquiring her magical aid.

When the princess entered the small cottage and found herself alone with the witch she immediately broke down into tears. "Sorceress!" she exclaimed. "I don't know what to do! I love a man who thinks of me only as royalty, and never so much as looks in my direction. I suspect he loves another, but I can't be sure, and I don't have the courage to ask. Oh please, is there anything— anything at all— you can do?"

As I've said, the Blue Witch was among the cleverest of her sort. She perceived right away what to do. Handing the princess a small vial of clear liquid, she said, "Take this, my dear, and give it to your love. Put it in his cup as you pour him tea."

"But what is it?" asked the princess.

"It is an honesty potion. When he drinks it, he will tell you all you wish to know, and you can satisfy yourself as to his availability. But wait!" The Blue Witch then tapped a few sprinkles of cinnamon into the vial. "It is a bitter brew," she explained, "and cinnamon will disguise the taste."

At that, the princess departed, much delighted to have her honesty potion. What she did not know, however, was that it contained no magic at all. In her cunning, the Blue Witch had given the princess a vial of plain spring water, adding cinnamon for reasons all her own.

Later that day it was the stableboy's turn. He made his way to the cottage of the Blue Witch. "Sorceress," he said. "I have need of your spells. Give me something to make another fall in love."

With an unreadable smile, the Blue Witch handed him a vial.

"Take this, my lad, and give it to your girl. Put it in her cup as you pour her tea."

"But what is it?" asked the boy.

"It is a love potion. When she drinks it, she will fall hopelessly in love. But wait!" As before, the witch added a few sprinkles of cinnamon. "It is a bitter brew," she explained, "and cinnamon shall disguise the taste."

The stableboy departed, much delighted to have his potion. But he too was deceived and carried no more than spring water in his vest.

The very next morning, as the stableboy brushed a horse in its stall, the princess appeared with a tray of tea. "You have been so wonderful with the animals," she began. "I wish to thank you, and share a cup of tea."

Seeing his opportunity, the boy quickly agreed, loosening the stopper in his own vial. "Allow me, my princess," he said in his most chivalrous voice, and then took the princess' cup from the tray. Secretly, he poured into her cup the contents of his vial, which of course were no more than spring water and cinnamon, then filled the remainder of her cup with tea.

"No, you must allow me, my good sir," said the princess, taking up the second cup from the tray. Into it, she secretly deposited the cinnamon water from her own vial, and then filled the remainder of the cup with tea.

The princess and the stableboy then stared across the tray, their cups upraised, and each offered a kind word before sipping. They drank. Like a mirror reflection, the two choked at once, each of them tasting cinnamon in their own tea.

Oh dear! thought the princess. *I have drunk from the wrong cup! Now I will bear the effects of the magic potion. And as it was an honesty spell, I will be unable to prevent my tongue's speaking, and will tell secrets I did not wish to tell!* Upon that thought, believing herself hexed by the tea, the princess revealed her true heart. She told the stableboy of her love, of her undying affection, and her desire to marry him should he consent.

But the taste of cinnamon was upon his lips too, and the stableboy had achieved a great panic. He thought, *Alas! I have somehow poured my potion into both cups! And truly it is potent, for the princess has already succumbed. It is only a matter of time before I fall in love with her too!* And upon that thought, believing himself hexed by the tea, the stableboy surrendered his wicked ways. He allowed the blossom of love to open wide in his breast, and agreed to marry the princess at once.

Of course the kingdom was now safe, having both a queen and a king. The evil sultan was thwarted in his plans. And the Blue Witch, to whose cleverness the whole kingdom owed all, returned to her kitchen to fill vials with spring water.

Now Tabetha, being a girl no less clever than the witch, had made this story as long as she could. She added far more details than were necessary to include here and so I gave you the short of it, leaving out the sultan's long, hateful speech and the Martian invasion and any number of descriptions that served no purpose but delay. For the overall effect of her story, which took roughly one hour to tell, was that of a perfect diversion.

"And what," asked the queen when Tabetha's tale was told,

"was the name of the clever Blue Witch from your story, the one whom you say saved a kingdom?"

No sooner had she asked than the sound of tramping feet could be heard. A sound that could mean only one thing. "I'm guessing," said the Mungling, "that her name was Tabetha Bright."

And as he spoke a thousand Gwybies stumbled in, already shaking with wild-eyed laughter. It appeared their Grimpkin guides had been fast at work.

Their queen, on the other hand, was slack-jawed with shock. Her eyes went back and forth between Tabetha, an eight-year-old girl in blue pajamas and a crown, and the strange army of monsters now rolling in the moss, shivering with fits of laughter.

"How did you do it?" asked the Queen of the Hollow with pure wonder, suspecting magic or treachery was involved, but Tabetha said only, "Thank you," and then, "We'll pass on the tea," for an empress must always be polite to her subjects.

The queen was befuddled, to say the least. Before she knew it she had offered Tabetha gifts: four empty goblets, one for herself and each of her friends, along with an escort of Grimpkin guides. So it was that Tabetha, the Mungling, Answer, and Isaac left for the Wink Hole to Arctus Ulai.

$\mathcal{C}$

Sometime later, among the mossy trails of the Hollow, they paused their march to catch their breath. The hum of evening insects fired up and the Mungling finally asked, "How *did* you do it, Tabetha? How did you even know Gwybies could laugh? I would have thought them rotten to the core."

Tabetha's strength felt paper-thin. She took another sip of fresh water from her goblet, set it down. "I knew it when I saw them swinging in the Great Hall." Then she added in a more thoughtful voice, "For all their wickedness, even Gwybies carry a little place for joy."

"Well, you promised a plan," the Mungling replied, "and it couldn't have worked better. Just think! You got rid of the Gwybies *and* Morlac in a single stroke!"

Tabetha massaged her knees. "I don't think so. The Gwybies, maybe, will never leave this Hollow. But Thomas will be safe. I bet he could drink a whole jug of that queen's tea without cracking a smile."

"You think he's that evil?"

Tabetha shook her head. "I think he's that sad."

$\mathcal{R}_\iota$

By now, the friends had discarded their magic frowns. Under orders from their queen, the Grimpkins were on good behavior leading Tabetha and her group through the woods. No pranks. No silliness. Nevertheless, they couldn't seem to avoid leaping and heaping and tumbling and stumbling, as if they knew no other way to move about.

Against the little men's urging, the group was forced to pause once more on the trail. It seemed the distance Tabetha could travel without stopping was growing shorter and shorter. So they made the most of their break, drinking more water and sharing a crust of black bread, even chewing heartily at a few strips of dried fox tongue. The Grimpkins were impatient to continue, but Isaac quieted them with a look. He had no intention of leaving until his empress was ready.

Which brings me to Tabetha, and the water she drank.

Now there are three things you must never, under any circumstances, do when traveling through the enchanted empire of Wrush. The first: Never tickle a troll, no matter how much he needs it. The second: Never feed him fried beans. But the third, and by far most important rule is this: Never drink from the cup of a frightened man, for in Wrush, you see, fear is more contagious than germs.

Ah, but so is real courage! And the will to do good! And for this reason everyone wished to drink from Tabetha's goblet. It was a beautiful goblet, quite fit for an empress. "But it's just water," she said when her friends requested a sip. "And everyone knows the last sip is all backwash."

Yet they savored the water, like men lost in a desert. Tabetha watched them, fascinated, as they filled her cup twice. When it seemed everyone had had their fill, Tabetha's friends sat quietly for a time, as if absorbing the fullness of her character from those sips.

The trail continued up the crease of a valley. At the far end they faced cliffs. The Grimpkins urged them up zigzagging trails, switching back and forth until they were high enough for a view.

But there was nothing to see. A mysterious fog had descended about them, little by little, until only the trail beneath their feet could be seen. It was so thick they could taste it. Their clothing grew damp. The only clue that they were at the top of these cliffs came from the Grimpkins, who finally called out: "The Wink Hole! Watch your step!"

Everyone staggered to a halt. Looking around, they found themselves in a featureless land, a land painted grey as smoke. They had been swallowed, it would seem, by a cloud. The Grimpkins grew nervous and backed slowly away. Tabetha heard them stumbling down the trail. Then she smelled it, a smell like spilt gasoline.

"It's close," Answer whispered, sniffing the air. But the Wink Hole, like a small fire at noon, remained invisible as ever. And no less dangerous for those who fell upon it unaware.

Tabetha breathed deep and felt a wetness in her lungs. She coughed and rubbed an ache in her chest. She could feel the otherworldliness of this place, an emptiness that yanked at her core.

"No, it's like this," she heard the boy-wizard say, and saw him demonstrating to Isaac how to find the Wink Hole by covering one eye. Tabetha did the same with the palm of her hand, and suddenly the Wink Hole appeared in the space beneath the thick fog. With one eye shut, she could see it clearly. A black pit. A burrow. A channel through space.

A dragon's doorway to Arctus Ulai.

Tabetha gazed down into the dark hole, imagining the great golden claws and long smoldering jaws that had burrowed from this world to the next. By Answer's description the Pump

Dragons were tremendous creatures, both in spirit and flesh, blessing all of Wrush with their wisdom.

Now the dragons were gone. Scattered throughout the universe in search of their Noble Trees. Tabetha wondered if even now they circled Earth the way moths do a lamp, looking for some way to get in. Hoping to find their fruit at the very heart of the universe. This was certainly the way Thomas had planned it. She knew he had destroyed their trees in Wrush to drive the Pump Dragons away, to drive them Earthward in search of their food. And that once he ripped down the Hedge, the Pump Dragons would tunnel through to Earth, with Thomas's army following in their path the way jackals trail lions at hunt.

"So who's going first?" she heard the Mungling say, staring with one eye into the Wink Hole. Last time it had been her, the most terrifying moment of her life.

"What will it be like?" asked Isaac, staring down into the hole.

"Just imagine," replied the Mungling, "jumping off a cliff at night. Then multiply that fear times ten."

"Then let it be me," replied the captain. "If there's danger in this, I'd rather be the one to find it." One eye covered, Isaac walked to the very edge of the Wink Hole. He turned, nodded once to Tabetha, and jumped.

The enormous pit swallowed Isaac and the sound of his last gasp. A moment later, there was nothing. Just blackness and an emptiness that could be felt more than seen.

Without a word of warning, Answer dove next. Headfirst, no less, and then he too was no longer in this world.

"That leaves us," Tabetha told the Mungling, her heart

pounding in her throat. She gripped the reins tighter as he scooted to the edge. "Are you as scared as me?"

The Mungling peered down into the bottomless hole and Tabetha leaned back for balance.

"Yup!" he cried, and the two of them plunged into darkness.

"Get back," said Answer, his voice dangerously calm.

A word to the wise.

Before jumping from a tall, tall building into a tiny dumpster far below it is important to ask yourself, "Am I being rash? Have I thought this thing through?" If, for example, there is nothing wrong with the building's stairs or elevator, you might want to take a moment to consider those routes. Do not let your decision be swayed by the suggestions of those people who will no doubt be gathering below.

Of course there will be times when you are in a terrific hurry, as all of us sometimes are, and jumping will make the most sense. If that is the case, then you must remember to drop straight down. If you follow your urge to push off from the roof as you jump, you will over-shoot your target, which is the center of the dumpster. Supposing you are lucky enough to hit your target, and it is filled with crash-friendly objects such as cardboard boxes or squid, you may even survive. Your chances are greatly improved by landing in a certain manner. I will teach you.

Once you have entered your gravity-induced descent— also known as *falling*— tuck your head and roll forward. You will want to do a three-quarters somersault. Somersaulting in this fashion is the only way to ensure you will land on your back, which is necessary, as in this position your body will naturally fold into a V (head to toes) when you hit.

As I am sure you understand, this advice is limited and does not extend to jumping into other dimensions and so forth. Tabetha, for example, benefited not at all from these suggestions as she plunged into the utter blackness of the Wink Hole. For her, the journey was like a very fast slide between worlds, on a chute made of silk and whispers. Tabetha glided through twists and glossy soft turns, her skin singing with tingling warmth. At the end of the tunnel, she and the Mungling pitched high in the air, twirled head over heels, and then slammed down like bricks into a bank of snow.

Tabetha gasped in shock. The cold stung her limbs. It took several moments just to breathe. She had been spit from one world to the next, like fizzy pop from a shaken can, and now lay aching and dazed. At last she rolled to one side and looked up. It was night. A frosty moon hung in the sky.

"Where am I?" she mumbled. Her thoughts came slow. Snow crunched under her elbow as she sat up. She shook the white flakes from her hair, rubbed the cramp in her thigh. Understanding struck like a slap.

I'm in Arctus Ulai.

She glanced around with new eyes.

The land of the second pyramid.

Before her lay a world of glittering ice and crisp silence, bright with wet light from the moon. From horizon to horizon it was smooth as a bottle, and so clear she could stare for miles— not outward, but *downward* as if peering into a ball of glass.

With a jolt of panic Tabetha patted her pockets, relaxing only when she felt the shapes of her salamanders. They poked out their little heads for a look around. *One of you here is about to help us unlock the next Puzzle Bead,* she thought, wondering which one, stroking the glow of their skin.

Isaac caught sight of her, crying "The empress!" He rushed to her side, his burly hands flapping like bird's wings. He brushed the snow from her shoulders and resettled her crown. "There now, were you injured? Is everything all right?"

Tabetha couldn't help but smile at this great bear of a man fussing over her like a maid.

"I'm fine," she told her captain with genuine warmth. Perhaps the only warmth, she realized, in this land of frozen glitter and ice.

She hugged herself against the bite of wind and the Mungling retrieved a fur cloak from his saddlebag.

"Just be glad it's not winter," he said, digging again through his bag. "Winters here must be unbearable. Believe it or not, Answer says it's still April on Arctus Ulai."

April? thought Tabetha. *Spring?* So far as she could tell, a lump of coal on a trampoline had more spring in it than April on this Mote.

"Uh-oh," said the Mungling, stopping suddenly with an arm shoulder-deep in his pouch. "I may have forgotten something."

"Something important?" Tabetha's teeth were chattering.

"I hope not." Reluctantly, the Mungling turned to meet Tabetha's eyes. "I didn't bring any paper." He gulped. "You have no way to return home."

Tabetha chewed her lip, nodded. It made no difference. Though she told no one else, returning to Earth had never been part of her plan.

"So where do we go now?" she asked, yanking the cloak tight about her shoulders. This wintry air made her chest ache.

Answer was already inspecting the Pyramid Map on the back of the Mungling's head, occasionally hissing at him to hold still. "Once again, the landscape of the map has changed," the boy-wizard declared, still staring at the Mungling's puffy scalp. "But that was expected. Nevertheless, looking at these markings, one would never guess we stood upon a speck of frozen dust."

And this was true. Nothing about this place suggested it was anything other than a planet. Tabetha marveled at the pulse of stars in the sky, like flickering tacks holding up the black felt of space.

"According to the map, we are to head for the Twilight Gates," Answer announced. "That must be where the second pyramid is hidden." With that, he whispered into the crook of his arm, and immediately four golden tattoos took flight. They circled high into the sky, paused like balls tossed at the moon and now on the edge of return, then burst like arrows of light in four different directions.

Tabetha waited. A small breeze stung her face and her nose ran. She was bundling deeper, tucking her chin to her chest, when Answer's tattoos came flashing and fluttering about her friends. They alighted on his arm and whispered in a language like crackling fire. Answer bent his ear to their words, then popped back up with eyes bright. "It's this way!" He pointed. Tabetha tried to follow his finger, but saw nothing. Nothing at all but glaring meadows of moon-soaked ice.

(decorative break)

Tabetha's eyes drooped heavily as she bumped along in her saddle. The Mungling's breath washed about her like ghosts. More than once, her mind slipped on the slick edges of sleep and she startled to find herself still on his back.

But this world was cold, so frosty it burned. Only the sting of this place kept her alert. She rubbed at her chest, which did little good. Her fingers were slow with numbness.

Suddenly, Isaac sprinted ahead a few paces and then halted. "I think I see something!" Tabetha perked up, and felt a sharp surge of excitement. "You see it?"

Isaac turned back to them. "Do you all see it too? Just over there. It looks like a light!"

It had begun to snow. Tabetha peered, her eyes straining to see through the huge, falling flakes. But off in the distance she thought she could see a light as well. Like a faraway emerald on the horizon.

"The Twilight Gates," Answer declared, "We've almost reached the second pyramid."

Still bare-chested, his eyelashes white with frost, Answer turned to resume their path. The boy-wizard trudged on, definitely hurrying now, and in his movements Tabetha sensed tension. She guided the Mungling to her wizard's side and asked what, exactly, the Twilight Gates were.

It took the wizard a moment to reply. "The Twilight Gates are a doorway, Tabetha. A doorway between light and dark."

"Should I be worried?"

"You should be careful."

He left it at that.

Within minutes, their destination loomed before them. Tabetha and her friends halted, staring, utterly bewildered. The Twilight Gates reared up, a pair of enormous doors, but there was nothing on either side or above them. Just two doors, all by themselves, twinkling in the middle of an icy nowhere.

Isaac ran behind the gates. "It's the same back here!" he cried. "There's nothing! Nothing at all!"

"Now that is strange." The Mungling made a slow sucking noise through his teeth. "I don't get it. What's the point of these Twilight Gates if they don't go anywhere?"

Answer, saying nothing, brushed falling snow from his brow.

Tabetha urged the Mungling forward. The mystery of these gates only increased. They appeared woven, top to bottom, from tiny strands of ice, the entire gateway as delicate as a spider's web. She stared at the oddity, wondering who built it, and how.

The snow tumbled and tumbled, and in the quiet of this place, Tabetha's heart suddenly began thumping like a rabbit. She had no idea why. But she was nervous, definitely nervous. Something was building, growing; a thick tension hung in the air. She looked quickly around.

Just snow. Everywhere snow, coming down like bleached leaves, but her feeling of worry grew stronger. Her ears began to ring from the pressure of it. A hum began pressing her skin.

The gates lit up with a ghostly swirl of green; no doubt the same light they'd seen from afar.

"Get back," said Answer, his voice dangerously calm.

"What? Is something—"

"I said get back!" he snapped just as two torches sprang to life, one on either side of the doors. "Get back! Now!"

The Mungling stumbled backward, Tabetha holding tight. Answer stepped between them and the gates. Without pause, he threw his arms wide and his tattoos sparked to life, ready to protect Tabetha from whatever came through.

The Twilight Gates creaked.

Answer stood straighter. Tabetha's breath caught in her throat. The doors creaked again, as though something strained from behind, something huge and powerful, something ready to burst through the gates. Isaac breathed heavily through his mouth, passed his sword between clammy hands.

All at once thunder roared, and the doors blew wide. Tabetha's ears popped at the sound. There was a terrific gust of color, blowing each of them down as though slapped by the aurora borealis.

Her hair whipping about her eyes, Tabetha squinted through the screaming haze and made out two enormous beasts lumbering through the doors.

The Twilight Gates slammed shut. The silence was immense, falling sudden and heavy. Tabetha could not help but stare.

"The *Drumpali Mund*," the boy-wizard muttered aloud. "Those creatures, those beasts, they are ancient protectors of the Shadow Key." The Drumpali Mund took up positions, like guardians of the gate, beside each of the bracketed torches.

Answer turned to Tabetha, his face a mixture of dread and awe. "I did not know, Tabetha. I suspected, but I did not know it would be them."

"What do you mean?" she asked. "What are you saying?"

She glanced nervously at the creatures before the gates. They stood huge and mighty upon two legs each, with long, shaggy white hair. Their snow-crusted shoulders were wide as large trucks, their arms hanging down to the ground. They would have reminded Tabetha of enormous gorillas in snowsuits if it weren't for their eyes. She feared them. She both feared and admired these creatures.

She said, "They aren't evil, are they. I can feel it. They aren't evil and yet, they're . . . they're dangerous."

The wizard nodded. "More dangerous than you could possibly imagine. These are the ancient keepers of the gates, and as such, are loyal only to the keeping. They are honorable. If you pass their test, they will let you through the gates."

"And if I fail?"

"They are honorable . . . but will not hesitate to punish. I'm afraid my magic can't help you here. Their power is far older than mine."

"Punish?" Tabetha felt the drawstrings of panic pull her heart tight. "I don't understand. What kind of test do I have to pass?"

Before Answer could reply, the Drumpali Mund shrugged the snow from their coats like winter oak trees shot through with a breeze. Upon their great lumbering feet, the guardians heaved forward. One crouched, holding before Tabetha a most extraordinary box.

Even the greatest of trials shall make diamonds of sorrow.

A box, I'm sure you know, is rarely remarkable in itself. It is what lies inside that makes a box worth noting. Not so with this box. It was woven of ice, just like the gates, and felt light as feathers in Tabetha's hands. What's more, this box held different items— always different, always changing— depending on the person who opened it.

Tabetha lifted the lid. Inside she found a harmless iron key. It felt small and narrow in her hand. But so too, I will remind you, would a piranha. Stranger still, this key was oddly shaped, as though twisted into loops at random, and printed with tiny symbols or letters.

"What is this thing?"

Isaac kept guard, never taking his eyes off of the two gigantic Drumpali Mund. Answer read the key's symbols from over her shoulder. He finished with a sigh, scratched his jaw before speaking. "It's as I both hoped and feared. What you hold in your hands is the Shadow Key, Tabetha. Known to me only in legends. It's not just a key to the gates, but a puzzle as well. Solve it, and the Drumpali Mund will let you through."

So this was her test. Tabetha looked at the strange symbols on the key once more. Then she looked to the doors and realized similar markings were engraved there. Why would that be? Holding the key up for the wizard, she asked, "Will you read it aloud?"

Answer's voice rang out like a bell:

There is bravery in light, and the brightness of day
But only through shadow will you find your way
Make peace with the night before a sunny tomorrow
And even the greatest of trials
Shall make diamonds of sorrow

"It's a riddle," said the Mungling. "Tabetha is great at these!"

But something about this riddle made her stomach clench. Her eyes drifted from the letters on the key back to those on the Twilight Gates. What exactly would the Drumpali Mund do if she failed?

She shivered at the thought. "Mungling, please take me closer to the doors. If we're lucky we'll find a keyhole there."

They drew closer, but no keyhole could be seen. Either it didn't exist, or the shadow cast by the doors prevented them from finding it.

Isaac and Answer appeared at her side. "Perhaps you need more light," the captain suggested. He went to retrieve a torch from the brackets, and Tabetha stared up the length of the gates, realizing the markings on them, and those on her key were not only similar but were in fact one and the same. The same riddle was written on both key and door.

Thinking, eyes closed, Tabetha heard the crunch of Isaac's footstep's returning. She then felt the heat of his torch and slowly opened her eyes, but what happened next truly startled her.

The symbols on the gates, so clear moments before, suddenly scattered like spiders from the torchlight.

"That was strange," she muttered, now staring at two doors without any markings at all. "It's as if . . ." She turned to Isaac. "It's as if we weren't meant to see them. By light, anyhow."

"That's ridiculous. How are you supposed to find the keyhole then?"

And Isaac was right of course. How *could* Tabetha find her way without light? Light was familiarity. It was safety and warmth. Light made things plain and clear while darkness, on the other hand . . . well, darkness was *dark*. It held secrets and dangers. It was the home of things unknown.

Tabetha thought back to the riddle.

But only through shadow will you find your way.

And in this one line she found the answer. That warm glow bloomed in her belly, stretching up into her limbs, and Tabetha realized it, too, had arisen from darkness. This glow had first sparked to life when she faced her fear of death, and grew bigger the more she made peace with it.

So how was she meant to find her way in the dark?

By trusting that tiniest light within.

"Put out the torches," she said.

"What?" her friends chimed.

"Please. Put out the torches," she repeated, and this time her orders were followed. Immediately, as if hatched from the gloom, the symbols reappeared, gathering into neat lines across the doors. Tabetha glanced again at her oddly shaped key. Her *Shadow Key*. Then back to the doors. She noticed something else.

"Answer," she said, "That symbol right there, what does it mean?" She pointed up high on the gates, to the second line of the riddle.

Answer stared up at the riddle for a long a moment, then slowly turned back to Tabetha. "*Shadow*," he said, a hint of amazement furling his brow. "That's the symbol for *shadow* you pointed to, Tabetha. But how did you know?"

She held up her key, and each of her friends fell silent. For when turned just so, the key's shape was that of the symbol. The key itself was the symbol for *shadow*.

And by the light of the moon, it cast a shadow of the symbol on the icy ground. It could be read there, so clear was the outline. Tabetha lifted the key so that its shade fell upon the gates, lining up the shadow from her key with the symbol on the door.

And it fit.

There was a great clanking and scraping, then a gust of warm wind.

The mighty Twilight Gates swung wide.

ℒ

Tabetha had passed the test. Her friends beamed with pride. She returned the Shadow Key to its woven-ice box, and with a tug of the reins, guided the Mungling toward the Drumpali Mund. They hunched motionless, their long white hair clumping with frost. Tabetha offered back the box and they nodded in solemn silence.

"Thank you," she said to them, then after a moment added, "for helping me make peace with the dark."

The Drumpali Mund each extended a huge arm toward the Twilight Gates, signaling Tabetha and her friends to go through. But no one moved. They were suddenly rooted with shock. What they saw did not seem possible.

"Bells and pumpkins," breathed the Mungling in awe. "Now *that* is some serious magic."

Answer nodded silently, his eyes glued to the towering doors. For when the mist cleared between them, this is what the four friends observed:

A city of ice. But it existed only beyond the doors of the gates. Looking to either side of the gates, no city could be seen. Nor was there anything but night sky above.

Once again, Isaac jogged around the side of the gates,

reporting that nothing of the city could be found. And yet there it was, right before Tabetha's eyes, as if she were looking at a picture come alive within its frame. It was daytime in there, as though she were seeing the backside of night, or someplace where everything in Arctus Ulai was reversed.

Tabetha focused her gaze. Through the portal of the doors she saw a bridge spanning a chasm, and just beyond that a high wall, the sort that wraps about a city like a fortress. Inside the city must have been a whole jumble of towers for their frosty spires could be seen above the ramparts. In there, too, would be a pyramid.

And beyond that, a task Tabetha could never share.

If only I could tell them, she thought. *If I could only make my friends understand.* Suddenly exhaustion crashed down on her like a ceiling.

Isaac returned, tugging his beard in astonishment. "How can this be?" he asked, glancing from the brilliance of the city to the emptiness of Arctus Ulai on either side. "It's like the difference between day and night!"

Answer chuckled softly. "With only the *Twilight* Gates between them."

Tabetha said nothing. Despite the excitement of discovery, she was truly struggling now. She was sinking into fatigue like quicksand.

"Come now," urged the Mungling. "I can feel Tabetha slumping in my saddle. Let's find this second pyramid and be done here."

The group passed through the Twilight Gates and emerged

in full sun. Their skin sighed at the first touch of warm air. Looking back over her shoulder, Tabetha saw the doors of the Twilight Gates were still there, but this time they framed the darkness of night.

"Stay close," advised the wizard. "You don't want to fall here." For like a bottomless moat that had been emptied of water, a gaping crevasse surrounded the city. The bridge across it was narrow, and slick with smooth ice. It arched over the deep gap without railings.

The group shuffled slowly across, hearts pounding like hammers. Only once did Tabetha look over the edge. Darkness. No bottom could be seen. This slender gorge may as well have split the world in two.

Tabetha exhaled in relief as they reached the far side of the bridge. A lip of ice, about the width of a road, ran between the gorge and the wall encircling the city. Its frozen blocks glistened with sunlight and moisture.

"This way! The city's through here!" Answer pointed to a second pair of gates set into the thick wall, leading through it like a lightless train tunnel. They entered. Momentarily hidden by shade, Tabetha brought a hand to her cheek. She felt the first flush of fever, and sighed. The burning shivers would not be far away.

Far ahead at the end of the tunnel, Tabetha could see the bright coin of day. It grew larger as they neared, and brighter too, making the tunnel seem all the more dark. Tabetha listened to the echo of their footsteps. She again felt the heat of her cheeks. Yup, this one was for real. There was no way to turn a fever like this back around.

"Everything okay?" the Mungling asked, and she mumbled an answer before distracting him with a question of her own.

"So if you had to guess," she said with some effort, "what sort of name do you think you have? I mean, you must have heard it spoken somewhere or another. Maybe you've turned toward a voice that was glowing in a crowd and then wondered later what had drawn your attention."

The Mungling sucked on a tooth, his steps clicking over unseen cobbles, his eyes focused on the point of light far ahead. "I admit I've had hints. Probably a hundred times or more, but like you say, Tabetha, each time I perk up my ears it disappears. My name is like trying to pinch a ribbon of smoke, or a word that falls apart on your tongue. For all I know, my name changes from one season to the next just like the Queen of the Hollow. After all this time, I'm not really sure I expect to find it."

"How long, then?" she asked. "How long have you been trapped, unable to return to your home in Earth's sun?"

The sun-wyrm stared absently ahead. "For as long as there has been a Hedge."

For some reason this made Tabetha sad. Far sadder than she would have guessed. It was as if those simple words opened a sluice in her heart. Every bit of grief she'd ever shut away came rushing out.

"I'm . . ." she swallowed, her throat burning and thick. "I'm so sorry to hear that, Mungling. I don't really know why."

The Mungling stepped clear of the tunnel and stopped. They were in a plaza, and he blinked in the bright sunlight glinting off the icy towers all around. Something was wrong. "Tabetha?" he said, his voice rising with concern. "Tabetha, what is it?"

But Tabetha couldn't lift her head. The fatigue, the sadness; both of them at once were too much. Her mother's last words were like an aching knot in her chest, and for an instant she no longer wanted to go on. What would be the point of all this after she's gone?

"Answer! Isaac!" the Mungling called out, and the two turned from the center of the plaza. "Tabetha's unwell!" The Mungling rushed her across, pausing only when he had caught up with the wizard.

"Tabetha, what is it? What can we do?" She heard the wizard's kind voice, but could say nothing in return. Her sadness was too deep and heavy. In her mind's eye she was alone in a limitless sea, and it was too much. Just too much for a little girl not to drown in.

She felt her life quickly leaking away.

She imagined her bed, tomorrow, some other child curled in its sheets. And then something very peculiar took place. Tabetha's pain was interrupted by that tender glow in her belly. A red rose of warmth bloomed within.

The glow sparked, and a single thought lit her mind. It was the last lines of the riddle on the gate:

And even the greatest of trials
Shall make diamonds of sorrow

Suddenly it was not Tabetha crying tears for herself there in the plaza, but the warm glow deep inside that was weeping. These tears were different somehow, as if the sadness was sweet.

A single teardrop hung from her chin.

Dropped.

Then stilled in midair.

Tabetha stared and sniffed at the tear in astonishment. Slowly, she reached out to touch it, then jerked her hand back. The teardrop had begun to spin. It blurred and flung light and Tabetha covered her eyes. When she looked again, it was not a teardrop but a jewel, and she understood how one makes a diamond of sorrow.

Before anyone could speak the teardrop rocketed up into the blue. An instant later the sky detonated rainbows. Tabetha and her friends tipped their heads back, eyes wide, for the sky had become a piñata spilling colors like candied hail.

"What's that sound?" she asked. It sounded like a faraway whistle. Something high above was descending at great speed.

The Mungling pointed excitedly at the sky. "It's your diamond, Tabetha! Zipping straight toward us, fast as a bullet!" The whistling grew louder, and everyone took a cautious step back. The whistling became a high whine.

"Everyone step back!" Isaac shouted.

Thud.

Tabetha jerked her shoulders in reflex just as her diamond struck the ice. It punched a tiny black hole in the crust. Answer, consumed by a wizard's curiosity, took a wary step closer. He bent to examine the hole, but startled when the ice around it began to snap. Answer stepped back, his face grim, watching cracks spread like slow lightning from the hole.

With doomed fascination the Mungling watched a crack thread between his feet. "Oh dear . . . oh d—" But the crunching and snapping of ice blotted his words. He began backing up with Tabetha in his saddle, the fissures growing longer and louder. Isaac scrambled out of the way. Answer stumbled backwards and fell, his eyes fixed on the hole as if it contained a bomb. And then silence.

Everything went still.

Tabetha held her breath, watched Isaac freeze in his tracks.

Answer brought a single finger to his lips, and . . .

CRACK!

Ice heaved into the air in an explosion of white, shards flashing and tinkling like glass. Tabetha tumbled from her saddle. Isaac shielded her with his body. Only Answer stayed put, one hand pointing at the hole. "Look!" he cried, then ducked his head instinctively against a puff of blasted ice. "Right there! Look!"

Isaac rolled to the side, allowing Tabetha a clear view. Where her teardrop had landed there was now a gaping fissure, and poking up through it was a tip. Distinctly triangular in shape. The pyramid! It was pushing up from below! It groaned and it hissed as it shoved its way higher. Ice popped like shots from a rifle.

"Come on!" Isaac threw Tabetha over his shoulder like a towel and rushed her to the safety of the plaza's edge.

They turned, looking on in amazement. There was a last CLAP! then a mist, then splinters whistling through the air as though the ice were applauding the pyramid's entrance.

"Actually," said Tabetha, "I mean to give you one thing more."

*O*n the calm that followed, Tabetha, still in Isaac's arms, gaped up at the icy slopes of the pyramid. The second pyramid. Home of the second mythic Puzzle Bead.

But the four friends had no time to admire this wonder. Immediately, Isaac rushed Tabetha through the pyramid's entrance with the others right behind. And just as quickly, the world changed before their eyes. Within the pyramid, they found themselves transported to the bustling kitchen of Tabetha's favorite Italian restaurant back home.

"This is where I always ask to come for my birthdays," she said, recognizing the restaurant's name stenciled across the white aprons and puffy white hats of the countless cooks hustling about. She always ordered a wood-fired pizza with pepperoni and pesto, and the cooks would place birthday candles on it and sing to her.

Everywhere Tabetha now looked, cooks were shouting and rushing, chopping and stirring. Steam sizzled up from a hundred boiling skillets. Unused pots dangled in rows above the stoves.

The Mungling, Answer, and Isaac, with Tabetha in his arms, all stood speechless amid the kitchen's narrow aisles. Though no cooks acknowledged them, they sidestepped the four friends as they hurried to and fro, platters balanced precariously in their hands.

Isaac carried Tabetha slowly down the aisle. She saw a ridiculously high mountain of dishes teetering in a sink full of suds. The man washing them glanced over his shoulder, just as Tabetha passed. She gasped to see the camel-faced man from the Hubbub Bazaar staring back at her.

"That man . . ." she tried to say, but Isaac didn't hear her, for at that moment a very tall, thin chef bumped her shoulder as he dashed by. She watched the tall chef speed away down the aisle. From beneath the back of his apron she saw a rooster's tale.

"Follow him!" she wheezed.

The rooster-faced man strode to the back of the kitchen, grabbed the silver handle of an enormous metal door, and stepped from their sight as he entered a walk-in freezer.

The four friends shared a look. In silent agreement, they followed the rooster, Isaac leading the way. He opened the large door, revealing a room clouded with mist. The icy bite of it stung their skin. Tabetha could see no sign of the rooster within. The white fog swirled about them as they ventured into the freezer. They moved deeper and deeper without any sign of a wall. The room seemed to have no dimensions or end.

Then a faint light appeared before them, and the friends waded through the mist until they came upon the cold gleam of a statue.

"There he is!" cried the Mungling. "Just like before!"

The statue was of Azu Prekahn, king of the Pump Dragons.

This time the dragon was carved from the purest ice. A strange concentration of light collected about him, so that he shone faintly in the whirl of whiteness. Rearing back on powerful haunches, with his dragon's wings spread wide, the look in his eyes spoke of otherworldly splendor. Here was a true king before her, of this Tabetha had no doubt. This was the legendary leader that would return one day and guide the last of the Pump Dragons to their Noble Trees. For a moment she remained still, sincerely lost in emotion.

Then she reached for the salamander in her left pocket. It was the blue one she withdrew, and he glowed like a bulb under cloth. She petted his neck and felt warmth. "There," she whispered in Isaac's ear, her eyes fixed upon the statue's chest. For above the scales of its heart was a keyhole.

Isaac pointed to the same, and she nodded. That was the place. He brought her near and she extended her hand. The blue salamander did not hesitate before crawling into the lock.

Immediately, he burst into blue flame and the icy carving of Azu Prekahn flickered with light. The pyramid's magic was unlocked and the dragon's jaws slowly opened. Isaac reached inside and withdrew what they'd come for.

"The second Puzzle Bead!" chirped the Mungling.

Like the first, it was about the size of a thimble and jagged as a puzzle piece on either end. "The Great Fang," said Answer. "Stolen from Azu Prekahn. You now have the second bead made from his tooth."

Isaac helped Tabetha remove the cord from about her neck where she wore the first bead.

Suddenly Answer's eyes went wide, as though Tabetha were reaching for the wrong end of a knife. "Be careful!" he blurted as she took the second bead in her hand. "Don't let the two pieces of the fang touch!"

"But why not?" asked Isaac. "They must be snapped together to destroy the Hedge, and Tabetha would never do that. Besides, all three pieces are needed, and we have here only two. Let her wear them both about her neck, if it gives the empress some strength. We all know she could use it right now."

The wizard sighed. "I suppose you're right. It just worries me, you see. After all these years, hearing legend stacked upon legend. You can understand why it makes me nervous just to see two beads together in the same room. It's possible that there is no more powerful object in the entire universe than those bits of tooth in Tabetha's hand. Go on though, Tabetha. Forgive me my fears. If anyone has earned the right to wear such power, it's you."

But just as Isaac slipped the cord with both beads over her

head, Tabetha's strength gave way. Completely, and all at once. It was as though she had been walking on thin ice, not just in Arctus Ulai, but all along. And her strength had finally fallen through to cold water.

She did not move in Isaac's arms. Her breath came ragged and wet. Isaac placed a cool hand on her forehead.

"She's burning up!" he cried. "It's her pneumonia!"

Tabetha saw real panic in his eyes. But in Answer she saw only deep sadness.

The boy smiled, ever so faintly, resting a calm hand on her cheek. "It's begun, hasn't it."

She willed a small nod.

The Mungling's eyes flashed nervously between them. "What has?" he breathed. "What has begun?"

Answer tucked a strand of hair behind her ear, then spoke the words that she couldn't.

"The end."

C

It is not a pleasant fact, this thing I am about to say, but it must be written here nonetheless. A sort of countdown had begun, back there in the second pyramid. The hourglass of Tabetha's life had been tipped.

She could hear only the huff of hard breathing as Isaac raced through the cold with her bundled tightly against his steaming chest. He was a desperate man, near mad with grief. Answer and the Mungling sprinted alongside him. Tabetha's

skin burned to the touch, but she felt no pain, sinking drows-
ily into the tranquil glow inside herself. She knew her friends
believed if they got her back in time, if they could only get her
to her medicine, then everything would be okay. She hadn't
the strength to correct them.

They sped back through the pyramid, through the icy city
of Arctus, and reached the Wink Hole at a full sprint. Nobody
slowed. Together, without so much as a pause, Tabetha's friends
leapt as one into its black depths. And for the first time, Tabetha
had no memory of her passage between worlds.

As if waking from a dream, she found herself surrounded by
toadstools. Only the heaving of Isaac's chest was unchanged.
Grimpkin's Hollow, she realized. They were back in Wrush.

And again they were running, running. Always running. She
closed her eyes and was asleep.

$$\mathcal{L}\iota$$

Answer's voice.

She woke and found they were still in the Hollow, but no
longer running. The giant mushrooms were clustered thick as
bamboo.

" . . .should have stayed on the path," she heard the Mungling
complain.

"Absolutely not." The boy-wizard thrashed ahead, blazing a
small trail. "It's hard enough to lose him already."

Tabetha licked her dry lips. Her voice felt like sandpaper in
her throat. "Lose who?" she forced out.

"She speaks!"

Everyone halted. Their faces gathered above her.

"Lose who?" she whispered again.

Isaac's voice was as gentle as her mother's. "No need to worry, My Lady. We won't let him catch up. We'll have you back in the Citadel in no time. There is paper there. Everything you need. All you'll have to do is write your way back, and everything will be okay! Do you think you can do that? Can you hold on that long?"

She licked her lips again. Swallowed. "Who's following us?"

"Thomas is. Thomas Morlac."

"Let him," she said.

"But why?"

"Are his Gwybies here too?"

"No," replied the Mungling. "Your plan couldn't have worked better. We passed them near the Spring of Mirth, you should have seen them! A whole army of monsters doubled over with laughter."

Tabetha tried to lift her head from Isaac's huge arms but felt nauseous. She slumped back against his chest. "Let Thomas follow," she whispered. "As long as he wants."

The Mungling clicked his tongue. "I don't know, Tabetha. We're not really sure what he's up to back there. He just keeps following along, maybe a hundred paces back. He never tries to get any closer. And he's definitely alone, but as mother Munglings always say, 'There's nothing so dangerous as one fool running from danger.' And I've seen it myself. A desperate person is likely to do anything."

"He won't hurt us." Tabetha closed her eyes again.

"How can you be sure?"

But she was already asleep.

She passed from dreaming to waking and back again as smoothly as a revolving door. At times she didn't know the difference. Her fever was alive. Her eyes would crack open, and she would wonder where she was. Before she could grasp it she was out again.

Then she heard water. Her head throbbed and her vision danced with white spots, but she managed to sit up in Isaac's arms.

"Where are we?"

She looked dazedly around, this place strangely familiar. Answer and the Mungling walked slowly towards a bridge. Her eyes jumped back to the water, to a river like melted gold, and with a tiny burst of elation she understood where she was.

Arrr-ooooOOOOOO!

Three silver horns lifted into the night air. Three steaming snouts bared fangs.

"We are the guardians of the Bridge of Conundros! No one may cross this river without paying the toll!"

Upon the bridge, filling it from rail to rail with his enormous bulk, a three-headed dragon towered over Answer and the Mungling, peering down at them with ruby eyes. It was the Thwork! Tabetha let out a small cheer inside.

Watching now from the edge of the forest, Tabetha saw Answer speak but did not hear what he said.

"Isaac," she whispered. "Quickly! Take me to the bridge!"

As they approached under the cover of darkness, Tabetha saw the Thwork spew angry smoke from his snouts. Ropes of slobber sizzled from his lips. "Enough!" the scarlet-scaled dragon roared, pointing a long claw at the wizard. "Speak no more of your wheedling words! I have been given the seeds to a mountain and a zebra's bold stripes! I've received lighting in a shimmering white egg! I possess the black tears of a Mud Fairy and an emperor's jeweled sword, but if you wish to cross this bridge, little wizard, then you must find and bring to me three gifts. Three gifts for your passage, and I warn you, if you can't—"

The Thwork's jaws dropped as Isaac brought Tabetha into view. "Tabetha?" the dragon hissed with a tight look of surprise, then all three of his faces lit with smiles.

"Tabetha! Why, it's Tabetha Bright! We've wondered what became of that clever little girl! Come now, come closer! Are these all your friends? You must forgive us our little speech back there, as we had no idea, and so many meals come to us in this way." The Thwork huffed a great laugh and bent down low. "Tabetha Bright! What a wonderful surprise. Now, what can we do for our favorite little girl in Wrush?"

"Little empress," Isaac corrected the Thwork. "It's your favorite *empress* you now speak with."

"Is that so?" The Thwork gave a look of delight. "Then we are honored as well."

Tabetha coughed, a raspy, painful sound. "We need to cross the Bridge of Conundros." She coughed again, and then managed the tiniest smile. "If you don't mind, that is."

"But of course!" the Thwork bellowed. "We owe you that much and more! You once gave us the one gift we couldn't purchase, the gift that makes a dragon whole."

"Actually," said Tabetha, "I mean to give you one thing more."

The Thwork shook all three of his heads. "Absolutely not. We simply can't accept. Don't you understand, Tabetha? You've *changed* us! Perhaps not in our taste for fine fare, but we see the world through new eyes. You paid the toll that no one else could, and you are free to cross this bridge as you like, whenever you like!"

"It's not for me," Tabetha explained. "It's for the next to come along. I'm paying you the toll for another."

"Another friend? Not a problem! Any friend of yours may pass. Just give us their name."

"Morlac," said Tabetha. "His name is Thomas Morlac." She saw tiny fires ignite in each of the Thwork's red eyes.

"I know Thomas and his Gwybies may have caused you trouble in the past," she went on, "but it's important to me that he crosses this bridge. Tonight. For payment, I offer you this . . ."

Carefully, for it was made of tender white petals, Tabetha lifted the Orchid Crown from her head.

The Mungling gasped. "Tabetha! No!"

She held out the crown for the Thwork.

"Tabetha, please!" the Mungling begged. "You can't give this up! Don't you understand what this means?"

Tabetha met his eyes briefly, tried to speak through the pain. "I do."

She set the crown into the Thwork's motionless claws.

Breathless, the dragon stared for a long moment. Then stepped from the Bridge of Conundros, and bowed.

ℒ

After crossing the bridge, Tabetha plummeted back into sleep. The few words she had spoken completely drained her. When next she woke, her pajamas were soaked with fevered sweat. Her head was ringing and buzzing. The buzzing gradually grew louder and clearer, until she understood the sound was not in her head, but was the music of countless insects. She felt the throb of their humming.

With great effort, Tabetha pried her eyes open. She was in a jungle, and it was familiar too, for she had come to this very place on her first journey to Wrush. Nearby rose the blocks of old ruined towers, lashed to the earth with green vines. Walls crumbled into heaps, statues turned to moss, and the long fingers of roots prowled the earth like knotted serpents.

"I know these ruins," she tried to say, but barely a whisper passed her lips. Her voice was muffled further by the cloth of Isaac's blue tunic. She meant to say it again, louder this time, when out of nowhere, a brilliant tiger flashed from the foliage.

It came straight for them, a bounding streak along the path. Answer stepped out in front and raised his arms. He whistled low and long, and a dozen golden tattoos peeled from his arms and spun in a broad circle before him.

"Heel!" boomed a voice through the trees. But the voice was not Answer's.

"I said heel, Elsewhere!" the great voice hollered again.

The tiger halted, resting back on its hind legs. Obediently, it sat cat-calm in the path and luxuriously licked the back of its paw.

As though blasted with wind, the forest's high canopy began to shake and then parted. A giant's head appeared among the treetops. His friendly face was framed by shaggy brown hair, and his nose was as big as a tree-stump. He crouched before the tiger and tugged him lovingly about the cheeks. The tiger licked the giant's hands with affection.

"I see you've met Elsewhere," said the giant, facing them now. His eyes were like calm water at night. "Sorry for the fright," he bellowed. "I'm afraid kittens of this sort can be a wee bit unruly. They often mistake friends for prey. But we're working on that, aren't we little Elsewhere?" The giant snuggled the beast. "My little Elsewhere, the only place you'll ever be found."

The giant stood now, his full height equaling the trees. "But Elsewhere or not, he makes an excellent scout. That's why I let him lead the way. And today, I can see, he's found exactly what I've come looking for."

At this, the giant peered in Tabetha's direction, and Isaac's free arm yanked clear his sword.

"Hold it right there!" her captain growled. "One more step and I'll dice you!" He waggled his sword tip at the tiger. "And that beast there. I'm not much for kitties that can swallow my arm whole, especially when they answer to ogres."

"Giants," corrected the giant. "Ogres are mythical beasts. Even children know there's no such—"

"Quiet!" interrupted Isaac. "The empress is ill! Can't you see we need to get her home? Now tell us what you've come looking for, or be on your way! We haven't a moment to spare!"

"Well that's just the thing," replied the giant, as polite as ever. "It's the empress I've come for. I know time is short, and nothing is certain. But as I said once before . . . *she really must meet my brother.*"

All at once, the night sky was lit with an electric-blue net.

*N*ormally, reader, when a tremendous giant blocks your path, takes hold of your child, and makes off into the black of night, it isn't much cause for joy. Indeed it might even cause some distress. But this is Wrush, you will recall, where all giants are noble, and this giant particularly so. Back in Book One he made a promise to Tabetha and the time had finally come to see it through.

Tabetha dreamed she was being carried into the mountains. She dreamed a fire smoldered under her skin. She dreamed of Pump Dragons, of salamanders, of an old friend in the night. She dreamed of Earth, the pain it endured each and every day. And she knew one thing still remained for her to do.

A breeze passed like a damp breath across her burning cheeks. It stirred her moist hair and gently woke her. She was in the mountains; it had not been a dream. Jagged peaks circled her like the points of a fence. She glanced up into the sky, which was cloudless and black, then down to the earth lurching beneath her. It confused her for a moment to know she was being carried, all the while watching her friends from a distance. How could this be? There was Isaac trekking up a narrow mountain path, Answer and the Mungling beside him. Then a brilliant orange tiger loped ahead and Tabetha remembered.

It was against a giant's chest that she nestled.

"Where are we going?" Her voice was weak, breathless.

"I am carrying you home."

"Mmmh," she murmured. That sounded nice. She didn't understand, or try to.

The giant stared up at a steepled peak, growing closer and closer with each footfall. He said, "I promised you long ago I would come back one day. I promised you would meet my brother."

"Will I?"

One. Two. Three steps more. "You already have."

"Mmmh," she murmured. That sounded nice. She didn't understand, or try to.

They approached a bend in the path, the steepled slope towering above. The giant glanced back over his shoulder. "Looks like you've got a very dedicated friend or enemy back there. He's been following us since we met."

Tabetha glimpsed a boy standing perhaps a hundred yards down the trail, watching them, just as they watched him. Even at this distance, she felt Thomas's pain. But she felt too like she was floating. Like her fevered limbs were made of air, and a wave of quiet crept over her like soft bedding.

The giant stopped, and Isaac and Answer stopped at his side. Looming before them were the slopes of a mountain. *So peculiar*, thought Tabetha, her mind drowsy and sweet, *that a mountain could look so much like a pyramid.*

ℒₗ

There are times, reader, and places too, in which a person feels certain there is magic. It is a rare feeling, mind you, and often overlooked. But had you been there, gazing up at this mountain, I am quite sure you would have felt its raw tingle.

It could hardly be ignored.

Tabetha felt herself passed down into the strong arms of Isaac. The giant drew himself up, then spread his hands before the mountain as though wishing to gather its greatness into a hug.

"Lo, my brother's mansion!" he bellowed. "The place each of you seeks without knowing. It may have no doors, no windows, nor walls. But it is home. The place all journeys end." The giant looked to Answer and the Mungling, then turned to face Isaac, at last peering straight into Tabetha's eyes. "And the place one last journey is to begin."

Tabetha felt soft and weary. She struggled to stay conscious, like a baby snug in her father's arms. She glanced up at the mountain, then across to the boy-wizard who was anxiously studying the back of the Mungling's head. Abruptly, the pair grew excited. She heard something about a "mark" and a "map" and then the Mungling let out a shout.

"This is it!" he cried. "It was in Wrush all along! The giant's brought us to the third and last pyramid!"

"That's all good and fine," Isaac growled, then glared restlessly up at the giant. "But what of the empress? She's burning up in my arms! You promised to help her get home!"

"All in good time."

"But we don't have any time! Don't you see?" Isaac cried. "She's dying! Right here! She's dying in my arms! If you don't get her back now she'll . . ." Isaac stamped away and began pacing in a frenzy. He whispered breathless assurances in her ear. At last he stopped and calmed, then drew in a deep breath. He fixed his eyes on the mountain, and said in a voice hard with resolve, "She has to go in, doesn't she."

The giant nodded.

"All right," Isaac sighed. "All right then. How do we do it?"

"Perhaps it's time we ask my brother," said the giant, crouching down before Tabetha. "He is the eldest of our kind, and would be here if he could, but his wanderings take him far and wide. No matter, he can be reached in spirit, for he has asked me to give you this."

The giant produced a satchel.

A leather one. Tabetha's fevered eyes grew wide.

With a mysterious grin, the giant said, "My brother says he has no more need for useless trinkets. Whatever's in this bag is yours."

Tabetha stared at the purse, the *Stone Tamer's* purse, numbly fingering the worn bronze of the clasp. She swallowed, forced three raspy words. "Where is he?"

"Oh ho! And one more thing!" The giant's voice dropped low. "He says you're right . . . Perhaps Bumble-Slumps are worth keeping around."

With that, he drew open the satchel's flap. Tabetha and Isaac peered within. Stars spread like jewels across an enormous black blanket. And Tabetha fell in, still clutched in Isaac's arms, and tumbled soundlessly through the reaches of space.

To the very ends of the universe and back they drifted, Isaac's arms like ancient tree roots about her. And it was like a dream, this drifting. She felt no passage of time. There was only floating and the velvet whisper of the Stone Tamer's voice in her mind.

Then the great mountain was before her, and in the mountain was a door. For the mountain was no longer a mountain but a pyramid.

"We're here at last," she heard Isaac mutter, his voice at once dreamlike and sad. "Just a little further, Tabetha, and you can finally go home."

The Stone Tamer's satchel had been a window through worlds. The last pyramid stood finally revealed, a radiant white against the soot black of sky. Isaac hurried Tabetha through the pyramid's gate and within.

As he crossed the threshold there was a puff of bright light, momentarily blinding the pair. As the light dimmed, and

Tabetha could again see, she looked wonderingly at the room about her.

It was her own room. They were in Tabetha's bedroom back home. There was her blue canopy bed, unmade, and her bookshelf along the wall. The messy dresser stuffed with her clothes. Atop it were pictures of her family at the beach, and a porcelain figurine of a wizard.

From downstairs came the muffled chatter of Tabetha's parents. She heard the familiar sounds of her father making breakfast.

"You know this place?" asked Isaac.

But Tabetha could only nod, unable to speak. For several moments, she simply let the feeling of this place fill her, a feeling so big her whole body ached. Then the sun peaked through her window and hazed the room with bright light. Craning her neck to the far wall, Tabetha saw her closet door was illuminated.

It now seemed long ago, but there had been a time when Tabetha was absolutely terrified of that closet. Each night, vividly imagined horrors had skulked behind the door: drooling monsters, moaning zombies, creeping creatures without names. None of which were real, of course. And yet Tabetha's adventures in Wrush had brought her face to face with much worse, proving she had within her, always, courage enough to meet every imaginable challenge.

As Tabetha gazed at the closet door, she could feel Isaac's breath quicken, and could even feel the beat of his heart.

"Open it," she said.

Isaac stepped forward and attempted to turn the handle.

"It's locked," he replied.

The door had never been locked before. Then Tabetha felt movement in her pocket, and was reminded of the last salamander. Slowly, with what little strength she had left, Tabetha removed the tiny creature from her pocket. It glowed a brilliant yellow in her hand.

"This is it, Tabetha," Isaac whispered in her ear. "After this it's all done."

Tabetha felt the dampness of the salamander's skin. She felt the eerie power within it. She lifted the salamander to the height of the door's lock, which grew before her eyes with dreamlike strangeness until it matched the size and shape of her salamander key. Then the salamander toddled across her palm and squirmed neatly into the lock. A bright flash of yellow, and then the lock sprung with a click. The door slowly creaked open.

Inside the closet was fathomless black. No light from the room could penetrate that gloom. Then from out of the blackness stretched a hand. It was the hand of a girl, though nothing of the girl's body could be seen. As Tabetha looked closer, she recognized the hand as her own. In the flat of its palm lay a bead. Tabetha reached out as the palm slowly turned, tipping the bead into her own.

The hand receded into the dark, and Isaac gently shut the door.

"It's done," he breathed. "You did it." Isaac sat down heavily upon her bed, as if discarding a load. He was finally free to share her exhaustion.

Tabetha said nothing. She gazed at the bead in her hand, the Puzzle Bead, the last of the three. She was almost too tired to think. Her eyes refused to stay open. She let them close, then heard Isaac's loud sigh. "The Hedge is safe at last, Tabetha. And you did it."

But she knew that she hadn't.

If she could only explain.

Finding the last Puzzle Bead was not her last task.

$$\mathcal{C}_{\iota}$$

"Tabetha? Tabetha are you awake?" It was the Mungling's voice.

She cracked open her eyes. She was back in Wrush, Isaac having carried her from the bedroom the same way they had gone, returning them through the magic satchel. Tabetha had slept through their passage and recalled only a dream of blue stars.

Tabetha now felt for her necklace and touched all three beads. Then from the cradle of Isaac's arms she gazed up at the mountain. It was again pyramid *shaped*, but no longer a pyramid *true*. The chamber within it was but a memory now.

Tabetha looked up into the faces of her friends. The Mungling smiled, yet his eyes were moist. Answer wore a look of grave sadness. Isaac held her close.

"The giant's gone." Her wizard struggled with these words. "I tried to stop him, Tabetha. I told him he'd promised. That he'd promised to bring you back. But the giant just smiled and . . ." Answer turned away. "He said you knew your way home from here."

Tabetha's skin was afire. Her head throbbed with thick heat. Almost, she thought. It's *almost all over.* She wished she could comfort her friends, tell them everything was all right. Through the murk of her fever she called out one name.

"Thomas," she croaked.

"He's gone, Tabetha. He's not here. I know you wanted him to follow, but we haven't seen him since . . ." The Mungling's voice fell short, and everyone turned at the sound, for out of the darkness emerged a boy.

"I'm here, Tabetha." Thomas strode to her side. "I'm here. And I've brought what you need. Take it," he said. In his hand he held out a sheet of paper.

"Tabetha!" cried the Mungling. "He's brought you paper! Quickly now, write your way back home!"

"Why?" she asked Thomas. "Why give me this gift?"

His voice became urgent. "Don't worry about that now. The Mungling is right. You have to write your way home!"

"But why?" she insisted

"Because you won, Tabetha. Because you saved the Hedge. And I made you a promise if you did. Now take it! Take the paper and write!"

"You." Her strength was fading. There was so little left. "You use the paper."

With a single, quick movement, Thomas removed a small object from his cloak. In his hand he now held his magic pen.

"It's out of ink," he said without feeling. "It's useless. I've no way back home. But you . . . you can still make it, Tabetha. If you go now, your medicine will save you!"

"You use the paper," she whispered again. To make her point final, she stretched out her hand, and gave Thomas her own magic pen.

"No!" cried the Mungling. Answer slumped like a landslide. "Tabetha, you've got to go back!"

But the pen was gone, a gift pushed into Thomas's palm. Something like a shock passed between their hands in the exchange. His eyes went wide, as though he'd been struck by lightning or wonder, and Thomas Morlac, I am overjoyed to announce, would never be the same again.

He could not be the same, for he had glimpsed the sun in Tabetha's heart, and now his eyes were forever etched with that image. The walls of his misery caved in and collapsed, a cloud of red dust and bricks. He understood that anger was a punishment all its own.

For Tabetha's part, she recalled Thomas in the window, a boy once blurry with light, and then again beneath the doors of her palace. This was the real Thomas, she knew, the one she'd always believed in. And here he was at last, her friend.

Deep in her belly, that warm glow grew to a blaze. It surged like a wave and engulfed her. With her last thread of might, she slipped the Puzzle Beads from her necklace, and amidst gasps of surprise . . . fit two of them together with a *click*.

All at once, the night sky was lit with an electric-blue net. A luminous grid bridged the horizon.

"The Hedge!" Thomas whispered.

"What have you done?" Isaac hissed.

Tabetha took the third bead in her hand.

"Tabetha?" It was Answer, his face filled with pleading and hurt. He glanced with horror at the beads in her hand. *Why?* he seemed to ask, and she would have told him if she could.

But some things you just can't explain.

Like this. *Click.*

"It's you," Tabetha said.

At last we have come to it, reader, that great event I first promised. The event that changed the world. In southern Wrush to this day they tell a story of the girl who rode dragons, and in the east and the west they tell countless other versions of her tale. But in Tabetha's last moments, there was only one person at her side, and so only one person who could speak the whole truth.

That person was Thomas. An awestruck boy who later came to me as a man, asking only that I write this story. If he had not, I believe no one would know the details of how things truly finished that night.

No one would ever hear what you are about to.

Recall! It was on that clear starlit eve, high in the jagged mountains of Wrush, that Tabetha Bright reassembled the Pump Dragon's fang. And in so doing, the Hedge—the ancient spell that had for ages guarded the Earth— was hopelessly and forever destroyed.

Upon the final *click* of that last Puzzle Bead, a sound so ordinary, so harmless, so much like a chocolate bar snapped, three things occurred, one right after the other. Events as transforming as when continents collide.

First, the night sky turned to liquid with a giant whirlpool in the east, a Wink Hole that yanked the blue lines of the grid into a swirling funnel. A terrific splash was heard, as though a ship had been dropped from the clouds, and the first of the mighty Pump Dragons burst through.

One after another the golden dragons appeared, heaving themselves through the heavens. Answer gasped, nearly choking upon the sight. Isaac clawed his beard in disbelief. But the Mungling . . . the Mungling was oddly quiet as he watched the dragons in the sky, his head tipped in wondrous recognition.

Tabetha remained in Isaac's arms. She spoke to the Mungling's darkened profile. "They've come for you, haven't they," she said. The Mungling simply nodded, his eyes fixed on the giant dragons wheeling above.

"They've come back." He turned to her. "And I know my name."

The second event occurred at that moment.

Tabetha leaned close to the Mungling, and slung her necklace about his neck. He now wore the completed Puzzle Bead, the lost fang of old Azu Prekahn.

"It's you," she said.

"It's me," he whispered back. At long last, the Mungling was free.

Tremendous golden wings groaned up from his shoulders. His chest creaked as its bones expanded and swelled. Magnificent golden legs stamped down on the earth and golden scales folded back in neat rows. The Mungling, who was none other than old Azu Prekahn, threw back his great neck and bellowed, a sound that echoed like whale songs in a valley.

Tabetha heard a chorus of distant bellows rain down from the sky, for the Pump Dragons at once knew their king. They began swooping and diving so close that their wind gusted her hair. Their song became her beckoning call.

"I have to go now." She wiped at one cheek, looking up at Isaac and then Answer. "I have to say goodbye."

They gazed back at her in stunned wonder, too astounded to speak.

"I promise you'll soon understand." She said goodbye once more and shared a last parting glance. For it was then, as the dragons swept by in parade, that the third and most memorable event took place.

Tabetha closed her eyes. This would be it. The glow in her belly was the sun. Dragons thrust past her in a shimmering chain, each merely inches away. Tabetha held out her hand. She smiled as their scales brushed her fingertips. Who would have thought a girl in a wheelchair could ride dragons? And without another thought, she took hold.

Tabetha was ripped from Isaac's grasp as though snatched by a train. The dragon whipped her skyward and rolled. She looked down, her teeth clenched tight. She was flying! With the very last of her strength, she clung tightly to the scales. She waved farewell to her friends far below.

The dragon released a grand bellow and pumped his wings twice. He hung in midair and then tucked. And Tabetha, young Tabetha, the girl remembered for this ride, left Wrush forever as she dove through the swirling Wink Hole in the Hedge.

$$\mathcal{Q}_{\mathcal{U}}$$

Far below, Answer cried out. Isaac stood speechless. Thomas went wild with sorrow. He sprinted to the Mungling, to old Azu Prekahn, Lord and King of all Pump Dragons. "Please!" Thomas wept. "Tabetha flies to her death! Carry me now and we'll save her!"

Old Azu bent low so the boy could climb on. Then with a roar that shook stones, he leapt. Into the sky they flew, Thomas clinging to his back, but Tabetha's dragon was swift. They saw her, a spot of blue on gold, swoop down through the funnel in the Hedge. She disappeared, and Thomas's only desire was to follow.

Through the spiraling funnel old Azu dove like a hawk, emerging in the sudden daylight of Earth. Home. They had crossed between worlds. Thomas looked down. He saw cities and trees, the broad shadows of clouds. Behind him, the sky was dotted black with Pump Dragons.

They follow their king, he thought, *just as I follow her,* and he bent his head to the wind. It tugged tears from his eyes till his ears were moist. His hands began to throb in their grip. "We have to hurry!" he yelled above the crash of the wind. "There's no way she can hold on much longer!"

℘

Which was true.

Tabetha clung to the dragon's curved back. The cool of his scales pressed her face. Her fingers ached red; her grip began to loosen.

Was it strange, she wondered, *or just plain magnificent that falling should feel so much like flight?*

℘

The moment Tabetha let go, old Azu bent into a dive. He swept underneath and caught her with a small thump, and Thomas clutched Tabetha to the dragon's spine.

She made no sound, no sign of movement at all. The boy called out to Azu Prekahn, "She's not moving!"

She began slipping from Thomas's grip. He struggled to keep her in close. "Take us down! Quick, I can't hold on!"

Old Azu bellowed with volcanic emotion. From behind, the sky filled with like songs. As Azu descended, the Pump Dragons wheeled on, circling their king high above.

Thomas peered over the dragon's side. Below, he saw a field, then a small hill of blue flowers. Old Azu circled twice and landed there. Thomas quickly slid down to the ground, Tabetha limp in his arms. "Tabetha!" He shook her, but she still didn't move. Flushed with grief, Thomas kneeled among the blue flowers and pulled Tabetha across his lap.

"Tabetha!" he cried again. "Tabetha, wake up!" Her face was so pale, so peaceful and clear. Thomas felt his heart squeeze. "Tabetha, please!"

Ever so faintly, she opened her eyes. Her head turned slowly to one side. She reached out her hand, her fingers brushing blue petals. She whispered.

"What's that?" Thomas threw his head forward trying to catch her hushed words. "Tabetha, please. I didn't hear what you said."

"Forget-me-nots," she breathed, as though they'd come there to name flowers. She closed her eyes.

And did not open them again.

$$\mathcal{C}_\ell$$

Silently at first, Thomas began to weep. Then his shoulders hitched up and down as he sobbed. He bent over her body, rocking to and fro. Guilt gripped his chest like a vice. A single teardrop raced to his chin, then slipped and fell. It froze in mid-air above Tabetha.

A voiceless whisper flowed through his mind.

Even the greatest of trials shall make diamonds of sorrow.

Then the tear splashed into the crease of her lips.

Thomas stared, stunned, at this broken girl across his lap.

"Who are you?" he whispered under his breath. Then he pushed back in alarm. He brought a hand to his mouth. The first root climbed straight from her chest.

A second root followed, sinking its fingers deep into the hill, and then a third and fourth, and then a stalk. The little green shoot stretched up toward the sky.

Thomas scurried backward in horror, a feeling that transformed quickly to awe, and then anguish, and then love, for a tree— yes a tree!—began spreading its limbs. Thomas ran down the hill to better view the phenomena but the branching of the tree outpaced him. He ran into the field, but had not gone far enough. He ran clear to the fence line and turned.

There, where a hill of blue flowers hunched moments ago, was a tree unlike any before. It was not just stunning, or beautiful, or colossal or grand. It was all of these things leaping for joy. There was no tree on Earth that could match it in glory, an entire forest all by itself.

Thomas's gaze fell to where little Tabetha had lain. He saw roots arching and diving among the carpet of shadow. But of the girl he left behind, he saw nothing. Just the trunk of a legendary tree. And the Pump Dragons, who flew so high in the sky they appeared to be tiny squiggles of light, bellowed songs of thanks for their Noble Fruit.

The end

Acknowledgements

The author of this book would like to acknowledge the wonder and creativity that exists within each and every one of its readers. It is his hope that you cherish such gifts, and never outgrow them.

About the Author

*W*ho is The Karakul?

A very good question. As an initiate of the High Council of Secret Libraries, we know he looks after many dangerous books. We know he spends a good deal of time traveling, researching faraway worlds. And we know he is an expert on Wrush. Other than that, we don't really know much at all. The Karakul has always been secretive.

A biography on The Karakul was reportedly begun some years ago, but as the biographer was a genie, and remains locked in a lamp, no one can verify whether a single page has actually been written.

The one thing that's certain is this: Despite his secrecy, The Karakul has been frequently popping up at schools and sharing his tales of magic with students. If you would like to request a visit to your school, or wish to learn more about The Karakul and the wondrous world of Wrush, simply go to: www.TheSecretWorlds.com